Chapter One

Olivia Marvell stood impatiently at the bottom of the steps in front of the Swan Academy of Theatre and Dance. She was surrounded by her friends Tom, Georgia and Aeysha. They were all peering down the road with expectant looks on their faces. They had just come from the café and they were stuffed full of toasted sandwiches, cherry almond cupcakes and hot chocolate, and were now looking forward to the first assembly of the new school year. Olivia and her friends were going into Year Nine and they felt very grown up. Tom had developed what Aeysha liked to call "the Year Nine swagger".

"I have not!" said Tom indignantly.

"You have," insisted Aeysha. "But at least it's cooler than the Year Eight sashay and the

Year Seven scuttle."

"I've never scuttled in my life," said Tom.

"Of course you have. All Year Sevens scuttle," said Aeysha authoritatively. As if to prove her point, two Year Seven newbies in their smart new olive and gold uniforms scurried by nervously, hoping that they wouldn't be noticed by Aeysha and the others.

"That's how I felt when I first came to the Swan," said Georgia. "I thought Year Nines were so grown up. I'd have died if one spoke to me. It's odd to think we've got so ancient."

"Speak for yourself," said Tom. "I'm like my mum, who always says that she's young at heart but just slightly older in all the other places."

Olivia's little sister, Eel, appeared at the top of the steps and pirouetted her way down them with dizzying speed and remarkable grace. At the bottom she curtsied to several passers-by. One actually clapped.

"If Miss Swan catches you doing that, she'll eat you for tea," said Aeysha. "You could really hurt yourself." Then she added affectionately, "Little show-off."

Eel grinned. "I know, I'm a *terrible* show

off. I just can't seem to help myself. Particularly now I'm in Year Four." She peered at the little group as she turned to go back inside. "I came to tell you that all the teachers are heading towards the hall. You'd better get your skates on or you'll miss the entire autumn term."

"I'd hate that," said Tom. "I love this term. There's always so much to look forward to, like Hallowe'en and Christmas."

"Mmm . . . skating at Somerset House," said Georgia dreamily.

"I went with Emmy's family last year. It was magic," said Eel. "We should have a Swan outing."

"You organise it, Eel," said Georgia.

"That's not fair," said Eel. "I'm only eight. People should organise things for me." She sighed dramatically. "But I'm probably the best person for the job. I so often am. I'll get Emmy to help me." And she danced away.

"Where *is* Katie?" asked Olivia, her forehead wrinkled with frustration. "The bell's going to go any minute and if she doesn't hurry up we'll all be late for assembly."

"Maybe we should have invited her to the café with us?" said Georgia.

"Liv did," said Tom, "but Katie said no. She wouldn't come to the Newbies' Concert yesterday either. Even though Miss Swan made a point of asking her."

"I think she's worried that people are going to stare and whisper behind her back," said Olivia.

"I can see why," said Aeysha thoughtfully. "Particularly after all the stuff in the newspapers about her dad."

"And when they kept going on about her being 'the disgraced *Sound of Music* child star'," said Georgia.

"It can't be easy coming back to the Swan after being excluded. She was such a queen bee before. Now she's going to feel just like one of the newbies."

"Worse," said Georgia. "People are going to be watching her like a hawk. The slightest slip and they're going to say she hasn't changed at all. She's just the same old, poisonous Katie Wilkes-Cox, who wants to be a star whatever the cost to anyone else."

"I want it now – and I want it on a plate!" said Tom, flicking back an imaginary lock of long hair in a scarily perfect impression of the old Katie Wilkes-Cox. After she'd left the Swan, Katie had redeemed herself by helping Olivia and the others save the school from the mostly criminal business activities of her bullying property developer dad.

"That's exactly why Gran said we should look after her a bit, at least until she finds her feet and proves herself," said Olivia, whose grandmother, Alicia Swan, owned the Swan Academy. "But everyone must know that Katie has changed, otherwise Gran would never have invited her back."

"There she is!" said Tom, spotting a small, slightly forlorn figure hurrying towards them, weighed down by a bag no doubt full of practice shoes and clothes.

Katie reached the steps and looked at them nervously; her hair was tousled from running, her pretty face was pale and her cat-like eyes were anxious.

"Hello," she said in a small voice. "I'm sorry if I kept you all waiting. I . . . I just didn't want to get here too early. . ." She tailed off.

Olivia gave her a smile and a quick hand-squeeze as the bell rang loudly.

"The new term is about to start," said

Olivia, her eyes shining. "Come on, everyone, or we won't get a good spot in the hall for assembly. Gran's got that gleam in her eye that makes me think she must have some exciting news."

Katie watched them move towards the door. She took a deep breath and followed them in, and was immediately caught up in a tide of people heading towards the girls' cloakroom. As she was swept along, she thought she heard somebody whisper, "Just look what the cat dragged in."

Katie felt as if somebody had punched her in the stomach. Returning to the Swan was going to be as difficult as she'd feared.

Chapter Two

Alicia Swan cast her eye over her pupils. She always looked forward to the start of each new school year. It was a fresh beginning and everyone was so bright-eyed and eager. She could feel the energy in the room fizzing and bubbling. If only she could bottle it, she thought. She loved the optimism of all the Swans and she delighted in the promise of a new year; every exercise book was fresh, nobody had yet failed a maths test, and upcoming auditions offered the possibility of roles rather than heralding the rejections that were an inevitable part of show business. She glanced at Katie, and noted how pale and nervous she appeared. It was going to be hard for the child, but Alicia knew that the Swan was the best place for her.

She looked in the direction of this year's Year Elevens, who would be taking their GCSEs next summer before leaving the Swan. Some would go on to further training at drama school, others to take A levels and maybe head to university, but a number of them would go straight into the profession. Kasha Kasparian had left only last term but was just about to release his first single. He was one of the lucky ones. She wondered how many of her current Year Elevens would still be in the business in six or seven years' time and how many more, worn down by the constant rebuffs and lack of success, would have given up. Alicia had just come from doing an interview with a magazine journalist who was writing a feature on stage-school kids. The journalist had been enthusing about the "overnight success" of so many former Swan pupils, citing the actor Theo Deacon, the singing sensation Amber Lavelle and the young theatre director Allegra Featherstone, whose promenade version of *Alice in Wonderland* had taken the Edinburgh Fringe by storm. Alicia had raised an eyebrow.

"In my experience, it generally takes at least fifteen years of hard graft in the business to become what the media loves to call 'an overnight success'," she had observed drily. "Many who come out of the Swan have been training and working since they were seven or eight."

Now, she clapped her hands together to signal quiet and the noise died away promptly. Will Todd's voice could be heard in the silence, saying, ". . . then she screamed cos I'd put mice in her—" He broke off as he realised that Miss Swan was eyeing him sternly, even though her mouth was twitching. Everyone laughed.

"Just make quite sure that the mice stay at home, won't you, Will?" said Alicia. "Now to business. Welcome, everybody, particularly all of you who are new to the Swan, but also to those of you who are returning for the new school year. I hope you are all ready to get down to some really hard work after the summer break.

"As I'm sure many of you are aware, the Swan Circus was a big success in Edinburgh this year and won both a Fringe First and a Herald Angel, as well as getting rave reviews in all the major newspapers and on many blogging sites. There was a lovely big feature in *The Stage* too.

Congratulations to everyone involved. I'm very proud of you all."

Olivia and her friends grinned at each other. Most people in the room had no idea how close the Swan Circus had come to complete disaster in Edinburgh.

"Congratulations are also due to Toby Bond, who has been cast in *Billy Elliot*, and Sisi Holman, who will be playing the young Cosette in *Les Miserables*. Sisi will be our eighth young Cosette."

Everyone applauded. The Swan had provided a steady stream of talent for the cast and chorus of the long-running musical that was known affectionately in the business as "The Glums".

"More good news. Will Todd will be playing the lead in the new *Dennis the Menace* series that starts filming after Christmas, which I'm sure everyone will agree is the most deliciously perfect casting."

The Swans laughed and clapped.

"And I'm pleased to say that most of the building work to extend the Swan is now completed, so there should be very little disruption this term, although there are still some snagging problems to sort out and decorating to do. I'm afraid there is more building work to come, though, as the ceiling of the theatre needs attention, but for reasons which will shortly become clear that will have to wait until next term. Fortunately I've been advised that it's not urgent.

"Auditions. The normal rules apply. No auditions for anyone whose academic work isn't up to scratch or whose behaviour is considered anything less than impeccable. I'm sure there will be plenty of opportunities over the coming term, and I know that some of you are already booked for panto. But there are some excellent roles in the offing including. . ." Alicia gave one of her famous dramatic pauses, and everyone in the hall leaned forward a little. ". . .the role of Zelda in the upcoming movie of the best-selling books. This is a possibility for all girls in Year Nine and above, although Year Elevens might want to consider the likely disruption to their GCSEs with filming starting in May."

A buzz of excitement ran round the room. *Zelda* was the latest high-profile children's series to be giving *Harry Potter* and *Twilight* a run for their money. Every girl in the room would love to get a chance to play the lead.

"Now, I know that not everybody will want or be able to work this term because of forthcoming mock exams, or maybe because they've already worked as many weeks as they're allowed to by law, but I do have news of an exciting in-house project. For the first time ever, we're going to stage our very own charity Swan pantomime in our very own theatre!" There were loud whoops. "It will give us a chance to show what we can do when we really pull out the stops, and we will of course be inviting lots of casting agents and industry professionals, so not only is it in a good cause, but it will be a great showcase for you and the school. There won't be any other major panto in central London this year, so I'm hoping ours will be a real draw. And I have every reason to think that it will because. . ." Alicia paused again. "Because the script is being written by Michael Marvell as a gift to the Swan, and the director Jon James has also very kindly offered his services entirely for free. We're also confident that several former pupils will make surprise guest appearances."

There was buzz of excitement around the room, like the low hum of a jet engine.

Everyone knew Jon James, who was responsible for a string of West End hits. Michael Marvell was Olivia and Eel's uncle, the older brother of their dad, the famous high-wire walker Jack Marvell. He was a hugely successful Hollywood screenwriter who had won two Oscars.

Kylie Morris had raised her hand. "Please, Miss Swan, who are going to be the surprise guests?" she asked.

"My lips are sealed, I'm afraid," said Alicia. "We don't want it all over the press just yet."

"Theo Deacon? Amber Lavelle?" persisted Kylie.

"I'm not going to tell you," laughed Alicia. "Not until it's all quite sorted. These people have commitments that they have to work around."

She didn't say it out loud, but Theo and Amber also had a difficult agent who couldn't understand why her clients wanted to work for free for a Swan charity show when they could be commanding mega fees elsewhere. But she felt certain that Theo and Amber's commitment was genuine and that it would all work out.

"All I will say is that I don't think you'll be disappointed," she added with a smile. There were squeals of excitement. The thought of acting on the same stage as Hollywood's most dashing star was too exciting for words.

Alicia checked her watch. "Right. It's time to go to your first vocational lessons of the term. Please make your way out of the hall in an orderly fashion."

She stepped down from the stage and was engulfed by the children as they headed towards their dance and acting lessons.

"Miss Swan, which panto will it be?" asked Georgia.

"*Cinderella*," replied Alicia.

"Ah," said Tom, looking at his friends and waving an imaginary wand. "You *shall* all go to the ball!" Then he gave Will a wink. "Maybe your white mice could get parts, Will. They can be transformed into ponies."

Alicia shook her head firmly. "I don't want those mice anywhere near the school," she said. "I hope you've heard me loud and clear, Will?"

Will nodded meekly. "Yes, Miss Swan."

"I love those *Zelda* books. It would be so mega to play her," said Kylie Morris dreamily as she tagged along with the group.

"I'd swap seven GCSE A stars for the chance to play Zelda any day," said Nicola

Stephens. "You'd be made for the rest of your career after that," she added sagely.

"Nicola, you know it's not as simple as that," said Alicia tartly. "I expect that's what Lucy Hare thought after she was cast in the remake of *National Velvet*." Lucy was a girl from a rival stage school who had been splashed all over the newspapers as the next big thing. She had delivered a very decent performance as Velvet Brown, but because the movie itself had been panned, she had then disappeared almost without trace. Somebody was rumoured to have spotted her at an audition for the chorus of a *Mamma Mia!* regional tour. "As you all know, nothing is guaranteed in this business. Least of all success."

"Here today, gone tomorrow," said Will Todd. Alicia pursed her lips at the cruelty of Will's wit, but she knew that what he was saying was true.

"What exactly do the producers want for Zelda?" asked Aeysha. "In the book, she's a real chameleon. A complete shape-shifter."

"Your guess is as good as mine. Unusually they haven't even specified hair or eye colour. Only age. So it's wide open. But at least it means that it's an opportunity for a great many of you." Alicia smiled at them before she walked towards her office. "It could be any one of you."

"It could be anyone," said Kylie, "but it better not be Katie Wilkes-Cox." There were a few murmurs of agreement.

"What do you mean, Kylie?" asked Aeysha sharply. "Katie proved she'd changed when she helped save the Swan. She deserves her place here."

Kylie shrugged. She could feel she had the support of several other girls in the group. "Maybe she does and maybe she doesn't. Maybe she only came back because she saw the Swan as her best chance of becoming famous. We know that's all Katie Wilkes-Cox *really* cares about. But I don't think she should get to audition for stuff until she's been here longer. It wouldn't be fair if she just waltzed back in and then snatched a starring role away from someone who really deserved it."

Aeysha smiled. "Someone like you, you mean, Kylie?"

Kylie looked uncomfortable. "Yeah, well,

maybe." She waved her hand around. "Or it could be any one of us. It could be you, Aeysha, or you, Georgia. How would you feel then?"

Chapter Three

Olivia and Katie were on their way to a lunchtime *castells* lesson with Pablo. *Castells* were like human towers. The strongest *castelliers* made the base, then everyone else balanced on their shoulders in layers until the whole thing looked like an enormous wedding cake. They required huge strength, skill and cooperation, and over the last two terms the Swans had been practising hard.

Olivia and Katie walked past the auditions notice board just a few metres from Miss Swan's office. Kylie Morris and her friends were hanging around near it. Some of them had clearly just come from seeing Miss Swan and others were waiting to go into her office. Alicia was holding interviews with all the girls who wanted to try for the role of Zelda. Katie's tap shoes made a sharp noise with every step she took.

"Hark! Is that the sound of someone prepared to walk over anybody to get what she wants?" said a sly voice. Olivia thought it was Kylie but she wasn't entirely sure. It could be any one of the six or seven identikit Year Nine and Ten girls who hung around whispering together about boys and make-up. Eel called them the Coven because of their fondness for black eyeliner and witchy comments. Olivia wasn't going to give them the satisfaction of reacting so she walked on pretending that she hadn't heard a thing. But she glanced at Katie and saw that she'd turned bright pink and was chewing her lip furiously.

"You shouldn't listen to them, you know," whispered Olivia fiercely as soon as they'd turned the corner. "They're just jealous because they know how talented you are, Katie. They see you as a rival."

"I know *exactly* how they think," said Katie sadly, "because I used to think just like them. I saw everybody else as a threat, one to be eliminated if necessary. It just hurts because Kylie used to be a friend, or at least what I thought of as a friend in those days. She even came on safari with my family. I never expected to be welcomed back with open arms after everything I did, but I did hope she and some of the others might be kinder. But I guess she liked me for my family's money, not for me, and I can hardly blame her. I wasn't very likeable. I upset so many people by being mean and spiteful."

"You can't beat yourself up forever," said Olivia seriously. "You're a different person to the one you were then."

"It's a relief you think so," said Katie. "The old Katie is dead and gone and I can't say I'm sorry." She sighed. "Although, of course, I do miss the high life. The theatre trips. The swimming-pool parties. The holidays in five-star hotels. So does Mum. After the house was repossessed and Dad fled abroad to avoid standing trial, she got really depressed. She hates having no money and she's having a really hard time adjusting. We've even had debt collectors at the door. Dad left such a mess behind."

"How is your mum doing now?" asked Olivia.

Katie flushed. "She's all right," she said,

and it was clear from her tone that she didn't want to discuss it further. Olivia felt embarrassed by her question. She didn't want Katie to think she was prying.

Olivia sat in Alicia's office with her feet twisted round the legs of the chair. Her lips were set in a mutinous line. Her grandmother gave a long, low sigh.

"I know you didn't put your name forward, but I wish you'd at least give it some thought, Livy. Not just say no outright. I think you'd make a lovely Zelda. So does Sebastian," she said, referring to the Swan's head of acting. "He says you've been working so hard in acting class. You proved in *Peter Pan* that you have the makings of a really fine actor, and there's no singing and dancing, so you don't have to worry about that."

"Is there any high-wire walking or trapeze work?" asked Olivia from beneath a curtain of dark hair.

Alicia tried very hard not to show her exasperation. "You know there isn't, Livy. Why don't you at least let me put your name down for the auditions?"

Olivia squirmed. It wasn't just that she didn't want anything to interfere with her high-wire and trapeze training. The thought of doing an audition made her feel sick. She couldn't understand why most of the Swans were so keen to put themselves through a process that as far as she could see could only feel like being a prize heifer at a cattle market, and more often ended in disappointment than success. She'd once asked the others why they did it, and Tom and Georgia had looked at her as if she was mad, and said that they really enjoyed auditions. Well, Georgia had said that she started to enjoy them once she'd got over the fluttery sick feeling in her tummy.

"It's no different from trying out for a football team," Tom had said. "I mean, some people are going to get in and some people aren't. And if you don't, you just have to get over it and try to get better."

Georgia nodded.

"But it's not quite the same, is it, Tom?" said Aeysha thoughtfully. "I don't know anything about football, but I'd guess that it's quite easy to see who is good at it and who isn't, but something like acting is much more subjective.

Even more so than dancing and singing. There's no obvious way to measure acting, and what one person thinks of as good acting might be total histrionics to another. So when you get rejected at an audition it feels really personal. I know it's just that you're not right for the part, that maybe you're dark-haired and they've decided they want a blonde, but that's how it can feel."

Georgia and Tom nodded vigorously. They both knew how it felt to be knocked back.

"If I'm honest," continued Aeysha, "Jodie, the girl I was up against in the final round of auditions for the *Tracy Beaker* movie, was probably a better actor than me, but on the day of the last audition, I had the luck and she didn't. So I got the role."

"But the point is that when you do get the part, you completely forget about the times you didn't. You feel on top of the world. Invincible," said Tom.

"Yes," said Aeysha. "But what if you don't ever get the part? You always just miss out. How would you feel then?"

"Well, if performing is what you really want to do, then I think that you just have to keep trying," said Georgia. "If you want it enough. If it's your dream."

Olivia remembered the conversation as she sat opposite her grandmother in Alicia's cosy office. She knew that she didn't want it enough. At least not now. Maybe she would in the future, but for now she wanted to concentrate on the tightrope and the trapeze. She had loved playing Wendy in *Peter Pan* for one night in the West End. She had loved how it had made her feel inside: as if somebody had lit a candle inside her tummy that was giving off a warm fizzing glow. But that had been an emergency. She hadn't had to audition, and she didn't even know it was going to happen until minutes before the curtain went up, so she barely had time to feel nervous. She just didn't want to try out for Zelda, even though she had read the book and loved the character.

"I know I'm disappointing you, Gran," said Olivia, "but I don't want to do it. It's just not right for me. Not now. I wish it was. I'm sorry."

"Oh, Livy," said Alicia softly. "The one thing I've learned over the last year is that you never disappoint me." Then she added with a rueful smile, "Puzzle me? Worry me? Frustrate me? Surprise me? Yes. But you never disappoint me." She gave her granddaughter a hug.

"Maybe it's not such a bad thing. Every girl except you is desperate to play Zelda. And so will every other girl in every other stage school and youth theatre group around the country. So there's going to be an awful lot of competition and there is going to be an awful lot of disappointment and tears."

"Gran," said Olivia shyly. "I would quite like to be in the panto."

"But you'd still have to audition for that, Livy."

"Oh, I don't want a leading role," said Olivia. "I thought maybe I could do some trapeze or wire-walking, although I doubt the theatre roof is high enough to rig. We would have to ask Pablo."

"I already have." Alicia smiled. "He's going to see what's possible and if the roof can take the strain. It is in a bit of a state."

"If not, maybe I could play the back end of the pantomime horse?" said Olivia. "That would be such fun. It would be mint."

Alicia watched Olivia leave her office. Her beautiful, serious granddaughter was so different from most of the other Swans. They were all so desperate for the limelight and eager for her to put their names forward for Zelda. She looked down at the next name on her list. This interview was going to be tricky.

Chapter Four

Olivia picked up her plate of pasta and salad and walked over to her friends' table. They were running through lines for a scene they would be playing together in acting class later that afternoon. They broke off as soon as Olivia sat down.

"So, why did Miss Swan want to see you?" said Georgia excitedly. "Are you going to go up for it, Livy?"

Georgia and Aeysha had already had their interviews with Miss Swan, who had happily put both their names on the audition list.

"Yes," said Olivia solemnly.

Georgia gasped.

"Liv Marvell, you dark horse," said Tom, shaking his head. "I'm surprised, but really pleased."

"That's amazing, Livy," said Aeysha. "I knew Miss Swan would want you to. Particularly after you were so brilliant as Wendy in *Peter Pan*. But I never thought you'd say yes. Not in a million years."

"Me neither," said Georgia. And she suddenly felt a bit funny, as if she was very hungry even though she had just eaten her lunch.

"Charming!" said Olivia with a smile. "I thought that you'd think it was a role I was born to play. Gran seemed to think so."

There was a little pause, and then Georgia said in a small voice, "Did she really say that?"

"Well, she seemed to imply I'm in with a very good chance, although she did warn me that I'd be up against some really stiff competition and so I wasn't to get my hopes up too high and end up being crushed."

Olivia could see Tom looking at her very closely and rather suspiciously.

"So, that means we'll all be up for it," said Aeysha. "That's going to feel a bit strange. Like being rivals. None of us have ever gone up against each other for the same job before. It's going to be weird."

"Oh!" said Olivia, sounding amazed. "Now I'm *really* worried. I hadn't realised you and Georgia were so keen to play the back end of the horse in the Swan panto. I may have to withdraw."

For a second there was a tiny silence as her words sunk in, and then Tom roared with laughter.

"Georgia, Aeysha, she's been winding you up. That's brilliant, Liv," he said, wiping the tears away. Aeysha started laughing too, and something like relief flashed crossed Georgia's face before she grinned broadly and said, "So you're definitely not going up for Zelda?"

Olivia shook her head.

"But, Livy, seriously, why aren't you at least giving it a shot?" said Aeysha. "You'd be great, I know you would."

"It's nice of you to say, Aeysha. But I just don't want to. I'll be keeping my fingers crossed for you and Georgia. I hope one of you gets it."

"We'll be rooting for you both," said Tom.

"Oh," said Georgia. "We might not even be called when they've looked us up in Spotlight." Spotlight was the huge database of professional actors that directors and casting agents used to find actors to play roles. "Anyway," she added gloomily, "even if we do get called I doubt we'll get past the first audition."

"Bet you will," said Tom.

"Even if we both do," said Aeysha, "in the end only one of us can be Zelda. One of us is always going to be the loser. In this business you're either first or you're nothing."

Katie sat in the same chair in Alicia Swan's office that had quite recently been vacated by Olivia. She was feeling nervous. She'd always felt that Miss Swan had the ability to see right through her. It made her feel uncomfortable, as if she had forgotten to put on all her clothes.

"How are you getting on, Katie?" asked Alicia kindly. The girl sitting in front of her looked so different from the sleek Katie Wilkes-Cox of old. In fact, thought Alicia, this new Katie may be less glossy, but she was actually far more attractive. Her work had improved too. Only the evening before Sebastian Shaw had said to Alicia that there was a new depth to Katie's acting.

"In the past I always felt that Katie was

acting being an actress. Now I get a sense that she really feels it and lives it."

"You're not seriously trying to tell me that hardship and misfortune have made her a better actor, are you?" snorted Alicia. "I thought you had no time for the silly notion that all good actors are damaged people in one way or another. You'll be telling me next that an unhappy childhood and being beaten four times a day is the secret to becoming a great actor."

"Wouldn't dream of trying," said Sebastian. "It's not a question of happy or unhappy childhoods. But whatever natural talent they have, all actors have to have some kind of inner life and emotional depths to draw upon. With the interesting ones there's always a feeling that what you see on stage is only the very tip of an iceberg, that it's all the intense stuff going on beneath the waterline that makes them really fascinating to watch."

"And does Katie have that?" asked Alicia softly.

Sebastian looked hard at her. "I think you know as well as I do, Alicia, it doesn't come along often. Sometimes you only see it a few times in a generation. Toni had it, and we've had a handful since, like Theo. At the moment I'd say that although we've plenty of talented children, we've only one pupil in the school for whom that's clearly true, and of course she's fighting it every step of the way, and by fighting it she may smother it until it withers and dies. But you know, I think there's a chance that Katie may be another. Who knows? It's a mysterious thing that often sprouts in the most unexpected places and in the least likely children."

"How do you think Katie's coping with being back at the Swan?" asked Alicia.

"Pretty well in the circumstances. Though she doesn't say much about it, I get the impression that things are a bit grim at home."

"Well, a lot of our children rise above their circumstances. Many of their families make great sacrifices for them to be here. She wouldn't be the first to have a difficult home life. I was really wondering how she is settling down in the school."

"Generally OK. Livy, Tom and their friends are keeping a pretty close eye on her. But I think some of the scarier Year Nine and Ten girls are doing their best to make her feel like an outcast."

"Ah, the Coven, as Eel calls them," said

Alicia with a glint in her eye. "I've noticed some of them are getting above themselves. I'm going to have to keep an eye on them. But it's understandable that some of them feel resentful about Katie being given a second chance."

"Eel's name for them is spot-on," said Sebastian. "It's a stage a lot of girls go through, but this gaggle are particularly irritating. But I reckon as long as most of them get a shot at Zelda and realise that Katie isn't getting any privileges she doesn't deserve at this stage, they'll back off and turn their attention to running each other down and discussing the latest miracle mascara."

After Sebastian had left, Alicia had been lost in thought. What he had said wasn't going to make her interview with Katie any easier.

But in the end Katie made it painless for her. The two of them had discussed how Katie was settling down and Alicia had praised her for the progress she was making in maths, and then there had been the tiniest of pauses before Katie suddenly blurted, "Look, Miss Swan, I know this is difficult. But I do realise you can't let me go up for Zelda. It wouldn't be right. I know it's not an option, however much I may want it."

Alicia gave a sad, kind little smile. "That's very mature of you, Katie, and very perceptive. I'm afraid it's quite true. I can't only think of what's in *your* best interests, I have to think of the whole school. It's such a pity the role has come up now, not next year. By then you would have proved to everyone what an asset the new Katie is to the Swan, but just at the moment I know that a number of pupils in the school will be alert to any suggestion that you are being given any special treatment. As far as I'm concerned, you redeemed yourself entirely when you helped save the Swan, but you made an awful lot of enemies before that and people can hold a grudge. So I'm sorry it's not going to happen for you this term. It's a shame; Mr Shaw says you're doing really well in acting class, and Miss Taylor has also been praising you for progress in dance class, and we all know that doesn't happen very often."

Katie forced a smile. She knew that Miss Swan was right, but she'd really hoped this wasn't what she'd say. Katie longed to have a shot at auditioning. Zelda was such a plum part. It would be well paid too, which wasn't the case with stage work. But then, after how she had behaved while in *The Sound of Music*, she knew it could be a very long time before she got a crack at the West End again. If ever. People's memories were long, gossip was rife in the business and forgiveness in short supply. Her dad's disgrace had raked it all up again. Her only real hope, at least for the next few years, would be in TV and movies. She wondered whether she ought to take a stage name. Katie Wilkes-Cox was what her dad would have called a "damaged brand", so tainted that she might never get another job, and if she didn't work at all over the next few years she didn't know what was going to happen to her and her mum. She wanted to be able to look after her.

"Oh well," she said a little too brightly. "It can't be helped."

"That's the spirit, Katie. I'm proud of you," said Alicia. "I'm sure we'll find something for you in the panto; not a leading role, of course. But prove yourself over the next year or eighteen months and I'm sure they will eventually come your way again."

"Yes, Miss Swan," said Katie, but her heart was heavy. A year or eighteen months was a lifetime. She wasn't sure that she and her mum could hold on that long.

As Katie slipped out Miss Swan's office she ran into Olivia and her friends walking down the corridor.

"Hi," said Aeysha. "How did your interview with Miss Swan go?"

"OK," said Katie in a small voice.

"Are you going up for Zelda?" asked Georgia curiously.

Katie gave a little laugh. "Of course not. It'll be the back end of the pantomime horse for me."

"Sorry, already taken," said Olivia with a grin. "I've bagged it. And Tom doesn't know it yet, but he's going at the front end."

"Aw, and I thought I was in with a chance of Prince Charming," said Tom in mock sorrow.

"In your dreams," said Olivia gleefully. "Although you might get a look in as an ugly sister."

"OK, I'll take the horse," said Tom. "That's if you're really serious about it?"

"I could say neigh," said Olivia, "but I'd be lying."

Chapter Five

Katie took some toast and jam and a cup of tea upstairs to her mum. They had run out of butter. She knocked on the door of the bedroom. The paint was peeling and the handle came off as she turned it. Katie sighed. She would have to ring the landlord and add it to the list of things wrong with their poky flat, like the boiler that delivered either scalding-hot water or no hot water at all, and the draughty old windows that rattled like loose teeth when the wind blew.

"Here you go, Mum," said Katie to the hump under the bedclothes. "I've brought you some tea. I'm off shortly and I won't be back until later tonight as I have an extra dance class with Miss Taylor. I've put money in the gas and electricity meters so you can have the fire on downstairs if you get up and watch TV. Maybe you could try and have a shower? There's a can of soup, some bread and a banana for your lunch, and I'll pick up some stuff to make pasta tonight on my way home."

The hump under the bedclothes didn't move.

"Mum," said Katie. "I know you're not asleep and can hear me. Please drink your tea and at least try to eat the toast. It'll make you feel better."

"Leave me alone," groaned the voice from the bed.

"Have you taken your tablets?" asked Katie. "The doctor told you that you had to keep taking them at regular intervals or they won't do any good."

"They don't do any good anyway."

"That's because they take a few weeks to kick in. You'll soon start feeling better," said Katie brightly, although she felt like crying inside.

"I couldn't feel worse," said her mother in a flat voice, appearing from under the quilt. "Oh, Katie," she suddenly sobbed. "What happened to our lives? How did it come to this?" And she waved her arm weakly at the dismal room with the damp patches on one wall.

"Things will get better," said Katie. But she didn't see how they could. When they had been evicted from their opulent mansion after her dad had left, Katie had appealed to her uncle, the theatre producer Chuck Daniels, to help them. He had sent a note expressing his sympathy but saying that he couldn't get involved. He had his career to think about. He offered to pay the rent on a cheap unfurnished flat for them for a year but after that they would be on their own. Katie tried not to think what would happen at the end of the year. If her mother didn't find herself a job she supposed they would be homeless.

But she couldn't worry about the future: she had more pressing things to deal with, including her mum's depression and the problems that had followed them from their old address. Almost every day brown envelopes covered with angry red writing poured through the letter box from creditors demanding money. No wonder her mum was depressed. If it wasn't for the Swan, Katie wouldn't have a reason to get up either.

She wondered whether she should phone

the doctor and tell her how worried she was about her mum. That she seemed worse not better. She glanced at her watch. She didn't really have time. She'd already got two misconducts this week for being late to school, and if she got another one she'd get a detention. She couldn't let that happen, as she barely had enough hours in the day even now. She thought bitterly about the old days when delicious fresh food appeared miraculously at every meal, the fridge was always full of treats and out-of-season strawberries and mangoes if she fancied a snack, and there was a constant supply of clean clothes and dancewear in her wardrobe. She had been ferried to and from school every day. Now she had to wash everything by hand, because even the launderette was beyond their means except once a week for the sheets and towels, buy and cook all the food and still keep up with her classes and her homework. It was exhausting. She caught a glimpse of herself in the mirror. She looked like a ghost.

"I've got to go, Mum," she said, and she dropped a kiss on her mother's head where it was just visible above the duvet. "I love you."

Her mum struggled to sit up. "I'm no good

to you, Katie. I'm sorry, lovely. I *am* trying."

"I know you are, Mum. We will get through this. See you later."

Katie ran downstairs, gathered up her bag and went to the front door. As she opened it, two sharp-suited men appeared instantly; they had obviously been lurking outside just waiting for somebody to open the door. Katie's heart began to hammer. She longed to slam the door shut, but then how would she get to school? From past experience she could hazard a pretty good guess that this unsavoury duo were either tabloid reporters or bailiffs. She'd had bad experiences with both. But these men didn't look like reporters. She felt relieved that it was her and not her mum who had answered the door. They couldn't come in if she was there alone. She prayed that her mum wouldn't hear the voices, but she doubted anything would rouse her.

"Can I help you?" she asked in her politest but steeliest of voices.

"Is your mum in?" asked one of men. "We need to talk to her." He flashed a piece of paper at her that had a name and "Debt Recovery Agency" written across the top.

"Sorry," said Katie smoothly. "She's out. Gone to work. She won't be back until really late."

The men looked at each other. The kid may be lying, but there was nothing they could do. "Mrs Wilkes-Cox! Are you there?" bawled one of them loudly.

"Will you give her this?" said the other man, shoving a brown envelope towards her.

"I can't take it. You'll have to come back another time," said Katie, eager to get rid of them. But luck was against her. Her mother, who so seldom ventured out of bed these days, suddenly appeared at the top of the stairs.

"Who is it, Katie?" she asked.

"Can we come in, Mrs Wilkes-Cox?" asked one of the men, while the other glared at Katie.

"You don't have to let them in, Mum," said Katie urgently, but it was too late. Mrs Wilkes-Cox had come down the stairs and opened the door wide. She waved them in as if welcoming guests to a dinner party.

The man shoved the envelope into her hand, and as she opened it and stared at the contents, he said gruffly, "You know what this means?"

Mrs Wilkes-Cox said nothing but nodded. She sank down on to a chair and said, "Do what you have to do. You will anyway. I'm too tired to try and stop you." Then she added bitterly, "I just hope it's worth your time and trouble. There's almost nothing worth having. It's all already been taken from us."

One of the men went outside and whistled for a third. Together the three of them looked around and began to remove items including the TV and the old sofa. Mrs Wilkes-Cox and Katie watched in silence as the men struggled to get the sofa out of the door.

After they had gone, Katie and her mum sat for a few moments looking at the room around them. It was now empty, apart from the table and the two wooden chairs on which they were sitting.

"Why? Why, Mum, did you let them in?" asked Katie fiercely.

"Because they'd only have come back again," said her mum. "I can't do this any more, Katie. I can't fight against it any more. It's like drowning. We're going to go under. Why struggle against it?" She looked at her daughter. "You better get off to school. You're going to be very late."

"I'm not going. I can't leave you, not like this," said Katie.

"You can and you must," said Mrs Wilkes-Cox quietly. "You're my only hope. My reason for living."

Katie dashed up the steps of the Swan. She had had to wait ages for a bus and she was really, really late. She scuttled into the girls' changing room to leave her stuff, hoping against hope that she might be able to sidle into her maths lesson without being seen.

She was heading up the stairs when she heard a voice call, "Katie Wilkes-Cox! Are you late again?"

Katie took a deep breath and turned round. "Yes, Miss Hanbury. I'm sorry, Miss Hanbury."

"Do you have a good reason?" asked Miss Hanbury.

"My bus didn't come," whispered Katie.

"That's not good enough. Other children manage to get here on time, and I'm sure many of them have much longer journeys than you. You must learn to organise yourself better and leave home earlier. Take a misconduct and I'll see you in detention tomorrow after school." Miss Hanbury stalked away to the staffroom.

"I won't cry. I won't cry," repeated Katie to herself like a mantra as she made her way to her maths lesson.

Chapter Six

Olivia and Tom were in a strange little cul-de-sac called Hangman's Alley a few streets away from the Swan. It wasn't somewhere they usually went. The alley was a dead end off another small side street called Henley Street, a gloomy, dank place with tottering buildings and warehouses, many of them half boarded up and in some cases overwhelmed by the curling tendrils of green creepers. The creeping tide of regeneration that was taking place down by the river hadn't yet reached this intricate maze of dark streets that looked straight out of a Dickens novel. Olivia and Eel had twice spotted a film crew there.

Olivia and Tom were trying out the little glider that Tom had made over the summer holidays. Tom was good with his hands and proud of the little aeroplane that he had painstakingly fashioned out of balsa wood and carefully painted.

"None of those plastic kits for me. All made from scratch," he had said proudly as he carefully lifted the glider from its box. Aeysha and Georgia had admired the aeroplane politely, but they weren't really interested. They were preoccupied with the upcoming auditions for the *Zelda* movie and had gone off to carry on reading the novel out loud to each other in preparation. But Olivia's eyes had lit up.

"Can we try it?" she had asked enthusiastically.

"I thought you'd never ask," replied Tom delightedly. He had been certain that Olivia wouldn't fail him. "She goes like a dream in the right conditions." Initially they had gone down behind the Swan but it was too exposed and windy. There had been a nasty moment when the glider had been blown into the branch of a tree and got caught there, and Olivia had to climb up with the agility of a squirrel and get it down.

"I think we'd better stop before it's

damaged or gets blown into the river," she said as she handed the plane back to Tom. There was disappointment in her voice. That was when Tom thought of the alleyway, which was protected from the worst of the wind by the tall, unloved buildings on either side. He and Will Todd and some of the other boys had sometimes kicked a football around there, although Will always said it was creepy and it often felt as if someone was watching them.

The alley was perfect for flying the glider, providing just enough wind for it to take flight, but also largely protecting it from the sudden gusts that had proved so troublesome down by the river.

"It's brilliant, Tom. You are a boy of many talents," said Olivia as she sent the glider sailing true and straight from one end of the alley to the other. "Do you think you could make a bigger version?"

"If I had the time. I like making things, and my dad says I'm good at it," said Tom. "But the Swan doesn't leave much time for outside hobbies. I'd never finish it. Even fitting in tightrope-walking is going to get tricky as we get higher up the school." He sighed.

Olivia looked aghast. "But you wouldn't give up the wire, would you?"

"No, of course not. I love it too much. But something has to give. You can't do everything."

"*I* want to do everything," said Olivia fiercely. "I want to walk the wire, fly on the trapeze at the Royal Albert Hall, learn to do stunts for movies, fly a plane into the eye of a storm, read the whole of *The Lord of the Rings*, climb Everest and find a recipe for chocolate fudge cake that never fails."

Tom grinned. "I bet you will too, Liv Marvell." He looked anxiously at the sky. "It's starting to get dark, and looks as if it might be blowing up a storm. We should head off soon."

"One last go," said Olivia, and she stood on tiptoe and sent the glider upwards. It caught the wind and sailed up through the air, but when it got halfway down the alley a sudden gust of wind tossed the little plane off course. For a second the glider looked as if it would plunge downwards and be smashed to smithereens on the road but just in time another squally gust gripped it. The plane veered to the right and the children watched horrified as it disappeared through the half-open top window of a crumbling building that was flanked by two apparently derelict houses.

"Oh, Tom, I'm so sorry," said Olivia.

"It wasn't your fault. It was the wind," said Tom stoically, but she could see he was upset. Olivia walked over to the entrance of the building. A brownish, mottled, double-fronted door was flanked by intricate plasterwork decorated with fruit and vines that would have been rather grand if the paint had not been peeling and the plasterwork chipped and crumbling. She rapped hard on the wooden door with her knuckles. The sound echoed. A shower of paint flakes fell at her feet like snow. There was an empty silence.

"It's no good, Liv. The place is derelict. It's obvious that nobody's been here for years. We'll have to let it go."

Olivia stood back from the building and appraised it. She thought that Tom was right about it being empty. The door didn't look as if it had been opened for centuries. The downstairs windows were shuttered and blind. Over the front of the building she could just make out some tired, faded writing that read "Campion's Palace of Variet". The last few letters were indecipherable.

She smiled. "It doesn't look much like a palace to me." She moved over to an old drainage pipe that ran down between the house next door and the derelict building and tugged it. It seemed secure. She reckoned she could shimmy up it and get on to the window ledge. Provided the ledge was sound she would be able to stand on it and maybe push the top sash of the window down far enough to climb in. She clambered on to a lower ledge and then on to the pipe.

Tom shook his head. "Don't even think about it, Liv," he warned. "It's not worth breaking your neck to get it back. It's only a bit of painted wood."

But Olivia ignored him. She pulled herself up the pipe as if it was no effort at all, swung over on to the ledge below the open window and tested it with her foot. It felt quite safe. She put her entire weight on it, stood up carefully and peered into the room. It was empty, with sepia-stained plaster walls and bare boards. She could see the glider lying near the door. She pushed down on the window and it gave easily. She looked down at Tom and grinned.

"Easy-peasy. Won't be a sec." She clambered over the top of the window and into the room, taking care to check that the dusty floorboards were sound. She walked lightly over to where the aeroplane lay, picked it up and was about to leave when she caught a glimpse of something and stifled a small scream. Then she realised she'd jumped at her own reflection in a tarnished gilt mirror in the next room. A trick of the light made her look like a little ghost.

"Liv! Liv!" Tom was calling her. There was a slight edge of panic in his voice because she hadn't immediately reappeared at the window. She took a reluctant step towards the window, but it felt as if something was drawing her back into the building. Looking beyond the doorway of the second room she could just see a glimpse of eggshell-blue paint, a touch of gilt and glitter. She thought she heard the sound of children whispering and laughing. She shook herself. She was imagining things. She wasn't frightened. She simply longed to go further into the building, but she didn't want to worry Tom. She ran over to the window and smiled down at him, waving the glider.

"Come up," she said. "It's really interesting.

We can explore."

Tom looked pained. "It really will be dark soon, Liv. We don't want to be wandering around an empty building in the pitch-black." But he saw the determined look on her face and, with a sigh, began to climb up the pipe until he could swing over to the window ledge and into the room. Olivia took Tom's hand and pulled him through into the house. There was something sleepy and enchanted about the place, as if it had been waiting for them to arrive and wake it up like the castle in *Sleeping Beauty*. They peered into one room and found an ancient carved mahogany bar. Bottles of spirits and empty glasses stood on the dark wood, laced with cobwebs.

They moved silently, as if pulled by an invisible thread, towards the room where Olivia had glimpsed the eggshell-blue paint. They stepped into it and both of them gasped out loud. They were standing on a horseshoe-shaped balcony supported by golden candy cane pillars. Huge, highly polished gilt mirrors set within large niches in the walls of the balcony reflected back the glitter of a thousand crystal drops that dripped from a vast chandelier, which hung over rows of patched burgundy velvet seats.

"It's a theatre!" breathed Olivia. "A forgotten empty theatre." And she and Tom turned to face the stage with its high proscenium arch and bare boards.

"It's so beautiful," whispered Olivia, completely entranced.

"It is beautiful," agreed Tom. "But you're wrong about one thing: it's not empty." He pointed towards the centre of the stage, where a single candle burned in a jam jar. "Somebody must have lit that. It didn't do it by itself." His voice was shaking. "Come on, Olivia, we've got to get out. I've got a feeling something bad, really bad, is going to happen."

Chapter Seven

Katie had almost finished writing her detention essay – "Why I Must be More Organised and How I Intend to Achieve It" – in the empty classroom. She was pressing so hard with her pen it was as if she was chiselling the words on to the paper, not writing on it. The pressure helped to relieve the mix of anger and despair she felt inside. She wrote the final sentence, "I really will try better in future." and leaned back on her chair to quickly read through what she had written. It would have to do.

She looked at her watch. Her hour was almost up. Miss Hanbury had sat with her for most of the detention but twenty minutes before the end she'd told Katie that she had an appointment.

"I'm trusting you, Katie, to finish your essay and wait until your hour is up. Then put it in my pigeonhole and sign out in the book with Mrs Gibbs in reception. She'll note the time so don't try and leave early because I'll be sure to hear about it." She had swept off, leaving Katie in the cold classroom by herself.

Katie picked up her essay, walked downstairs with it and posted it in Miss Hanbury's pigeonhole. She collected her things from the cloakroom, checked that it was dead on the hour and walked into reception. There was no sign of Mrs Gibbs but she was clearly around because the email she was in the middle of writing was still open on her computer screen. Katie's eye was drawn to the words "Zelda Auditions". The email was to someone called Poppet at the film production company. Below was a list of the names and mobile numbers of all the Swan girls who were being put up for the role. Mrs Gibbs was transferring them from a handwritten list made by Alicia and she had almost finished.

Katie felt a pang that her name would never appear there. She looked at the clock. It was getting late, and she still had to go to the cashpoint and get out some money on her mother's card so she could go to the supermarket on her way home. After that she would cook a supper that her mother would barely touch, and then she would have a pile of homework to do, and some lines to learn for acting class tomorrow.

She wished Mrs Gibbs would hurry up so that she could be signed out and go. She didn't dare leave without Mrs Gibbs' signature because otherwise Miss Hanbury would be on her case in a flash. She looked at the clock again and wondered how many buses she was missing. At least she could save some time by going to the machine a few doors up from the Swan and get that done while she waited for Mrs Gibbs to get back. She dumped her stuff by the desk, got her purse out of her pocket and went to the bank. The street was deserted. She put in her mum's pin number, carefully protecting it with her hand, selected cash and twenty pounds. It was, bar a few pence, the last of the money in her mum's account until Thursday, which was two days away. She knew it was going to be tough to make it last. It had turned colder, and the gas and electricity meters seemed to eat money like ravenous tigers. She needed to buy soap powder for her dance kit and washing-up liquid for the dishes too. There was almost no food in the flat.

She took her mum's card out of the machine and tucked it away in her purse for safety while she waited for her cash. She sensed movement behind her as two crisp ten-pound notes appeared out of the slot. She went to take them from the machine before she was roughly pushed aside. A man grabbed the money, turned and ran, dropping one of the notes in his rush to escape. Katie screamed, but there was nobody around so no one heard her or came to help.

Her hand was shaking badly as she bent to retrieve the ten-pound note. The man could have hurt her. Her eyes misted with tears as she walked back to the Swan and she wiped them fiercely away. Her mind was in overdrive. Just ten pounds to last two whole days! How would they manage? She couldn't bear to tell her mum. She was too fragile. She wished she knew if there was somebody you could ask if you ran out of money. She was sure Miss Swan would know. But she was worried that it would appear as if she was begging. As it was, Miss Swan had given her a scholarship so she could come to the school, and that even covered her uniform and practice clothes. She didn't want to seem ungrateful. Besides, she didn't want anyone at the Swan to know how desperate things were at home. The Swan was her haven, and she didn't want that to change.

She walked back into reception. Mrs Gibbs was still not around. Katie swallowed hard. All luck seemed to be against her. She felt like one of those people in the old Greek myths she used to love so much who the gods had cursed and who experienced misfortune at every turn.

She knew her mum was relying on her but everything seemed to be set against her. Well, she thought fiercely, she wasn't going to be beaten. She would just have to make her own luck. She moved in front of Mrs Gibbs' computer and looked at the screen. The open email was still there. It felt as if it was teasing her. She listened hard. There was no sound of Mrs Gibbs' approach. She leaned over the keyboard, moved the cursor higher up the long list of names that Mrs Gibbs had already typed and six names from the top she inserted the name *Kate Carmichael*, putting her mobile phone number next to it. She then moved the cursor down the list to where it had been hovering just under Georgia's name.

Katie felt a rush of fear, and all her fury drained out of her. She was being an idiot, she knew, dicing with her own future. She'd never get away with it, and she was in danger of destroying all the trust that Miss Swan had put in her. She moved back towards the keyboard intending to delete the name, but at that moment she heard the distinctive sound of Mrs Gibbs' high heels approaching.

Mrs Gibbs looked flustered when she saw Katie.

"I quite forgot that I was supposed to sign you out when you'd finished your detention. Miss Swan called me to her office and we got talking. I'm sorry, Katie. Off you go." She looked at the clock. "I must just finish writing this email and get off myself, or I'll miss my train."

Katie gathered her things slowly. She felt the urge to shout "Stop" and confess what she'd done. But her mouth was dry and she felt shaky.

Mrs Gibbs' fingers were flying over the keyboard. "There! All sent," she said with a smile at Katie, and she began to shut down her computer. Katie walked down the steps of the Swan in a daze. She didn't know whether to laugh or cry. She felt both exhilarated and appallingly guilty.

Chapter Eight

"Look!" said Olivia pointing at the stage. "A tightrope. It's as if it's there specially. Just waiting for us. Let's go down."

"Don't be dumb, Olivia. We need to get out of here," said Tom brusquely. But Olivia had already disappeared through the door into the gallery looking for a way down to the auditorium and the stage. Tom chased after her and as he did so, he felt as if someone had run a finger down his spine. He shivered and caught up with Olivia as she entered the auditorium. Her eyes had a slightly glassy look as if she was in a trance. Tom could feel his heart thumping inside his chest. He was sure they were being watched.

"Come on, Liv, let's get out of here," he

whispered urgently, and took her hand. It felt fluttery in his, as if he was holding a small bird. But Olivia didn't move. It was as if she was hypnotised. She was staring at the candle in the jam jar and the high-wire and the painted backdrop behind it of dark, mysterious woods with a distant turreted castle as if she was trying to work something out.

"It's so odd," she said wonderingly. "The rest of the building is crumbling away, but the theatre itself is still perfect as if somebody has been looking after it with real love. Look! The mirrors are polished. There's not a speck of dust. The seats have been patched and mended. The stage is set and ready. I bet the stage machinery works too. It's as if the entire place is stalled in time and is just waiting for an audience to appear and a performance to begin."

"Well, I don't want to be here when it does," said Tom firmly, glancing nervously over his shoulder. "Come *on*, Liv. We shouldn't be here. Whoever owns this place is going to be furious when they find us wandering around here without permission." But Olivia had run up on to the stage and tested the wire with her hand before leaping on to it.

"Liv!" he hissed. "*Liv!* Come down. It might not be safe. This is definitely one of your stupider ideas." She didn't respond. Tom shivered again. He felt as if Olivia couldn't hear him. She had a look on her face as if she was listening to someone or something far away. Tom sighed. The sooner she did what she wanted, the sooner they could get out of there. He climbed up on to the wire too. Tom wobbled a little, but Olivia moved with a fluent grace, almost dancing along the wire. Her pleasure in being in this beautiful space made her laugh out loud and her face was so radiant and her laughter so infectious that for a second it made Tom forget his fear and he laughed too. For a tiny fraction of a second he thought he could hear children giggling with them, but then it was gone. When Olivia met him in the middle of the tightrope, she flipped on to her hands and raised her legs for Tom to catch. As he did so, they were both suddenly caught in a spotlight. Tom gave a little screech, but held his balance as Olivia swiftly returned to an upright position.

"That's it, Liv. I'm going. I don't like this place. It's definitely haunted." Tom dropped awkwardly off the wire, eager to be away.

"All theatres are haunted, but some more than most," said a quiet voice from the front of the gallery. "That's why we keep the ghost-light burning. To let the ghosts know that we have not forgotten them and never will." The children, blinded by the spotlight, stared upwards into the gallery but could see nothing. Olivia jumped off the wire and ran to Tom and clutched his hand. Tom was quite pleased to find it was clammy. For all Olivia's bravado, he clearly wasn't the only one who was scared.

"Arthur! Lights, please," came the woman's voice again. The spotlight disappeared and a few seconds later the huge chandelier blazed into dazzling, brilliant light. The entire theatre blinked and sparkled. A second or two after that, an elderly woman appeared framed in a doorway at stage level and made her way slowly to the front of the stage. She had tears in her eyes.

"My babes in the wood have found their way home," she whispered to herself. "Lizzie and Davey, have you forgiven me, my lovely girl and boy? Please tell me you forgive me. I never meant to hurt you. If only I could turn back the clock before it struck midnight."

Olivia and Tom looked at each other. Was this old woman mad? Was she a ghost?

"Actually," said Olivia very gently and trying to keep her voice from shaking, "we're not Lizzie and Davey." As she said it, she thought she heard the tinkle of children laughing, the sound of running feet and a girl calling, "Davey! Davey! You can't catch me!"

"Did you hear that?" she asked Tom sharply.

"Hear what?" said Tom, eyeing Olivia anxiously.

The old woman's eyes widened and she took a step towards them. She looked fragile, as if her bones were made of feathers and her skin of parchment. She was wearing an old-fashioned evening dress and a feathered diamanté cap. Suddenly her mood seemed to change, and not for the better. Her eyes clouded with suspicion and she pointed a bony finger at them that made Olivia think of a witch in a fairytale. Then she cried, "What are you doing here? Why have you come? Spies. Spies! Lock the doors, Arthur! Call the police! They've come to steal my inheritance. They've come to close us down! Trespassers and thieves . . . trust nobody . . . you only get hurt . . .

lock your heart . . . keep love out. . ."

She was becoming more and more agitated. Olivia and Tom were really frightened. The old lady's face drained of all colour and she looked as if she might be about to have a heart attack. There was the sound of feet on the stairs and a man a few years younger than the woman stumbled into the auditorium and put his arm around her shoulders protectively and rubbed them soothingly.

"Calm yourself, Ella. They are not spies. They're just a couple of kids. They mean no harm."

The woman peered at Olivia and Tom through misted eyes. Her anger disappeared as quickly as it had arrived. "You children are from the Swan theatre school, aren't you?" They nodded. "I've sometimes seen you boys playing football in the alley. I like to watch you all playing."

"I'm sorry, we're trespassing," apologised Tom. "We didn't mean to. We thought the building was abandoned and empty. We only came in to retrieve my glider. It accidentally flew in one of the windows."

Olivia still appeared to be in a daze. "It's

so beautiful," she said suddenly. "It's the most beautiful theatre I've ever seen. It's magical. Is it yours?"

The woman beamed, delighted by Olivia's pleasure in the theatre. She put out her hand graciously.

"Ella Campion," she said, "of Campion's Palace of Varieties," and she gave a low curtsy. "And this is Arthur. Arthur Tuttons, the best stage manager in the business. There's no one to touch him, not even up West in those fancy theatres and nightclubs." She snorted disapprovingly.

The man nodded pleasantly at the children. "Don't mind Ella. She can get a bit confused. Lives in the past a bit. Other times she's sharp as a pin. But you'd never hurt a fly, would you, princess?" He gazed at her with such affection that his eyes shone. "What are your names?" he said, turning back to the children.

"I'm Olivia and this is Tom," said Olivia. She took a step forward and almost knocked over the flickering nightlight.

"Mind the ghost-light," said Arthur. "We don't want the whole place going up in flames."

"What exactly is a ghost-light?" asked

Olivia curiously.

"It's a light always kept lit in a theatre so that the ghosts can see to perform when the actors are not on stage," said Ella.

"Is this theatre really haunted?" asked Tom nervously. Ella fixed her sharp eyes on him and there was something cloudy and sad lurking in their bottomless depths.

"All theatres are haunted, if only by the spectres of all the performances that happened there long ago. One performance is never like another; it's an ephemeral thing. And it can never really be captured, even on film. You have to be there to really see it. No theatre is ever completely empty either. Its walls echo and whisper with lines from scripts delivered by long-dead actors, the cheers, applause and laughter of audiences no longer with us and the music played by orchestras who have fallen silent. It is always waiting, waiting to be full again and come back to life. In the meantime, we keep the ghost-light lit to welcome the ghosts so they won't curse us and they can play and laugh on the unoccupied stage."

The old lady seemed to slip into some reverie of her own. Olivia heard a sudden gurgle of children's laughter. "Davey. Davey. You can't catch me."

Olivia whirled around. "What *was* that? Is there somebody else here? Some other children?"

Tom gave a nervous little laugh. "You must be hearing things, Liv."

But Ella eyed Olivia very thoughtfully.

"You children look as if you need some tea. Will you join us?" She waved an arm. "There are trunks full of old costumes. Even a pantomime horse somewhere. You can take a good look. It would be nice to hear the sound of children within these walls again."

Olivia's eyes were shining. A pantomime horse costume! It felt as if fate had brought her and Tom to this strange, magical place. Tom clearly wanted to get away as soon as possible but Olivia said loudly and firmly, "Thank you, we'd love that. I just need to text my gran and tell her we won't be back for a while."

Chapter Nine

"Ella Campion? Surely not?" said Alicia, frowning. "She must be long dead."

Olivia and Tom shook their heads. "She's not. She's very much alive," said Olivia. "But she's ancient. Maybe ninety or even a hundred. Do you know her?"

Alicia laughed. "I know I must seem very old to you, Livy, but I'm not quite that old. No, Ella Campion was in the business long before my time. Campion's closed down before I was even born. I can't remember the details, but I think that something bad happened. Some kind of tragedy. You should look it up on the Internet. I can remember my grandfather telling me about Campion's when I was a girl. It was famous and Ella Campion was a legend. She was running

Campion's before she was twenty and that must have been during World War Two. She put on everything, from Shakespeare to variety and pantomime. Of course, Campion's was originally a music hall back in Victorian times when her family first owned it. I think part of the draw in its latter days was that it had remained much as it was, almost untouched since the nineteenth century. But it must be over fifty years since it closed. After the war people didn't want that old kind of entertainment. They wanted cocktail lounges and American crooners. There was a West End club my parents used to go to when I was a child. The Glass Slipper. It was considered the height of sophistication. I don't think places like Campion's could compete."

"Campion's Palace of Varieties," said Olivia, rolling the words around her tongue with pleasure. "Ella said that in her grandfather's day it was a bit like the circus. There were trapeze acts and high-wire walking as well as cancan dancing and even a performing horse. I'm not sure if she meant it was a real horse or not."

"It might have been real. In the nineteenth century the old Hippodrome in Leicester Square had novelty acts like polar bears and tigers, and the Alhambra had real waterfalls on stage. My great-grandfather used to go there at the turn of the twentieth century. The toffs came over in their carriages from the West End. It was considered a bit naughty because you could see the chorus girls' ankles, which was considered rather shocking in those days.

"To think Ella Campion's still alive! How did you meet her, Livy? She's a living piece of theatre history."

Olivia shifted slightly uncomfortably and shot a warning glance at Tom. She wasn't sure her gran would be pleased to hear that she had been climbing into apparently derelict buildings. She thought maybe it might be better to sidestep the question.

"Oh, Tom and I just sort of bumped into her in Hangman's Alley," she said as casually as she could.

Alicia frowned again. "I wish you children wouldn't hang around there. It's so bleak and isolated with all those boarded-up old buildings, like a ghost town," she said. "Still, it's nice to think that old Ella is alive and well, even if Campion's has long bitten the dust. It's a pity the way all that old theatre history and buildings have been lost, swept away by new flats and office blocks. Such a shame."

Olivia was about to interrupt her and explain that Campion's Palace of Varieties *was* still there in all its glory, but then remembered she might have to explain about getting into the building in the first place. She decided to wait until they had been back to Campion's to see Ella a few more times. Then perhaps they could take Alicia round as a surprise. She couldn't wait to see her grandmother's face when she saw the perfect theatre and the stage machinery. Ella and Arthur said it was all in complete working order even though it hadn't been properly used for years.

Alicia was still talking. "We should invite her to the Swan. She could come to see the pantomime."

"OK, we will," said Tom. "I think she might like that. She knows about the Swan. But she doesn't go out much. She looks as if a gust of wind might blow her away, and she seems to get a bit confused at times."

Alicia opened her mouth to ask some more questions so Olivia quickly interrupted with one of her own. "Gran, do we have a ghost-light in the Swan theatre?"

Alicia smiled. "Of course, all theatres do. It's that little bulb in a wire cage stage left. The one that's always on very low."

"So does that mean the Swan theatre has its own ghost?" asked Olivia, wide-eyed.

Alicia laughed. "Has Ella been filling your head with spooky nonsense? Theatre is such a superstitious business. We haven't got a resident ghost like so many old theatres claim to have. Some even keep a couple of empty seats at every performance, even the sold-out ones, in case the ghosts put in an appearance and want to see the show. It's considered bad luck if they turn up unexpectedly and there are no seats for them. It's the same with the ghost-light. It's supposed to make the ghosts feel welcome. It's all superstition of course. The real origin of the ghost-light is so anyone walking on to a dark stage doesn't blunder into the orchestra pit or trip over the scenery."

"Oh," said Olivia, disappointed.

Alicia laughed. "I'm afraid it's not nearly such a romantic explanation."

"Have you ever seen a theatre ghost, Gran?"

Alicia shook her head. "I reckon that you have to believe in ghosts to see one, and I'm a committed non-believer." Alicia looked serious for a moment. "Now, did Pablo find you? He says it's not possible to rig the theatre for trapeze, and even tightrope-walking will probably be impossible for the panto."

"Yes," said Olivia. "He told us earlier. He says the roof isn't strong enough. It's a real shame about the circus stuff, but never mind, there's still the panto horse."

Alicia frowned; she was quite surprised that Olivia had taken the news about the rigging so well, and she hadn't realised her granddaughter had been serious about being the back end of a pantomime horse.

"But, Livy, I've read the script and *Cinderella* doesn't have a pantomime horse in it."

"Trust me," said Olivia, dancing away with a grin. "It will do." She looked at the clock on her phone. "Gotta go, Gran. Come on, Tom, we've got to meet a man about a horse."

Alicia laughed. "OK, you mad twosome," she said, before remembering something else. "Actually, before you go, I've been meaning to ask you about Katie."

Olivia and Tom turned round slowly.

"I don't want you to tell tales," said Alicia. "But how's she getting on with the other children? I'd like to know if things are really bad. I have had brief words with one or two who I thought might be giving her grief, but I want to be certain she's not being singled out."

Alicia stopped. She could see from Olivia's face that her granddaughter felt awkward, and she hated that she had put her in a difficult position.

"Katie's a survivor, Miss Swan. She'll be OK," said Tom brusquely, who like Olivia didn't want to be seen as a snitch.

"I'm sorry, clearly this is tricky for you," said Alicia. "But I ask because the last couple of days I've got the distinct impression Katie wants to confess something to me but can't quite bring herself to do it. I wondered whether she was being badly bullied, or if things had got much worse at home and she can't cope. But if she won't tell me what's worrying her, I can't help her."

She gazed hard at Olivia and Tom. "If somebody's being bullied, it's not snitching to say, you know."

Chapter Ten

Katie stood in the wings waiting for her turn to audition. She was the very last person on the list and only Olivia and Tom were left to go before her now. Her heart wasn't in it but she had no choice because Miss Swan had insisted that Katie put her name forward for the panto, saying that it would be good experience for her to get up in front of her classmates and audition. "You've got to do it sometime," Alicia had said kindly. "Best to get it over and done with." Katie wished that it hadn't arrived quite so quickly.

Miss Swan clearly didn't realise just how horrible Kylie and some of the other girls were being to her. Not in any big way: they just weren't giving her a chance, but were dropping snide remarks and pretending she wasn't in the room when she was. Small-kid, primary-school stuff, really. When she had been the Queen of Mean she had been far more inventive in her nastiness. She'd had a special talent for it. There probably wasn't a person in the class, particularly among the girls, who she hadn't hurt or humiliated in some way. Now they were getting their own back on her. She knew it would probably pass, and she also knew she only had herself to blame.

"I'm not taking no for an answer, Katie," Miss Swan had said. "I've already added your name to the list of auditionees for the Swan panto. You deserve your chance, and I have complete faith in you."

What was far worse than the taunts from the other girls was the gnawing feeling that she had already failed Miss Swan by doing something utterly stupid and unforgivable. How could she have added her own name to the Zelda audition list without thinking through the consequences? Every time Katie thought about it, it made her stomach churn. If only she could turn back the clock. She was sure to be found out and then all the faith Miss Swan had in her would be destroyed. Katie would be excluded from the Swan for a second time, but this time forever. There would be no coming back again.

Katie took a deep breath as she watched Georgia finish her song and dance. There was only one thing for it. She was going to have to confess. If she tried to explain what had happened at the cash machine and how upset and worried she was about her mum and their lack of money, and beg for forgiveness, maybe Miss Swan would understand and show her mercy.

She had already tried twice, but the first time Mrs Gibbs had appeared with an urgent call for Alicia, and the second time she had just completely lost her nerve and had been left stuttering in front of Miss Swan.

But she wouldn't be such a coward again. The minute the audition was over, she was going to knock on Miss Swan's door and insist on speaking to her. She would confess all about her moment of madness, and get her name removed from the Zelda audition list, and maybe it would all be all right. Maybe her place at the Swan would be safe after all, and she'd make Miss Swan so proud of her that the Coven wouldn't dare come near her.

Georgia finished her audition and

everybody clapped hard, and a few people cheered as she left the stage and slipped back down into the auditorium.

"OK, Livy and Tom, let's see what you can do." Jon James, the director of the Swan pantomime, looked expectantly at the empty stage. He tipped back on his chair and yawned. It had been a long day. The auditions for *Cinderella* had started first thing in the morning with the youngest children in the school and were now finishing with Years Nine and Ten, who were sitting patiently in rows and watching each other perform. Everyone wanted to win a role in the panto.

The children had prepared their auditions without help from the Swan staff, even the very youngest ones. Some had performed alone, while others had performed in pairs or small groups. Eel, Emmy Lovedale and some of their friends had devised a wickedly comic spoof of *The Dying Swan* that had made Jon laugh a great deal and mentally vow to find a spot for all of them in the pantomime. He'd also enjoyed a high-kicking chorus line choreographed by Kylie Morris and some of her friends. But he had also heard endless renditions of "When I

Grow Up" from *Matilda* and seen scores of tap dancers, and although they were all highly professional, he was beginning to flag. He could already cast the Swan's *Cinderella* ten times over and inevitably some of the children were going to be disappointed, particularly as the major leads were going to go to ex-Swan pupils. Abbie Cardew, who was in an upcoming movie, was playing the fairy godmother. Theo Deacon had said he would play the prince and Amber Lavelle was going to play Cinderella. It was a pity really; Jon would have much preferred Olivia as his Cinders, but even if she would do it, which he doubted, she would be far too young to play opposite Theo.

It was a pity Theo couldn't be persuaded to play Baron Hard-Up or one of the ugly sisters. But when he and Alicia had suggested it to Theo's agent Sheridan, she had raised her eyebrow and said it would never do for Hollywood's most sought-after romantic lead to be laughed at.

"I have to think about Theo's future, darlings. He's not a Z-list reality-show celeb desperate to do panto, he's a real star *and* a serious actor. It's just lucky for you that filming on his new movie was put back and there was an unexpected gap in his schedule or he wouldn't be able to do it at all." She smiled so that big white teeth could be glimpsed behind crimson lips, putting Alicia in mind of a shark that had just had its tea. "You've got to remember he could be earning thousands elsewhere while he's helping you out on your little panto."

Jon had felt Alicia stiffen in the chair next to him and prayed that she wouldn't say anything. But she'd been so astonished at Sheridan's breathtaking rudeness that she was stunned into silence, although on the way back to the Swan she'd done such a perfect imitation of Sheridan that Jon had been in stitches.

"I know it's wrong of me to even think it," said Alicia, "but if anybody should play an ugly sister it should be Sheridan. She's so demanding and unpleasant, it would almost be typecasting."

Jon had smiled. "Maybe that's one of the things that makes her a great agent. Remember she did salvage Theo's career after he did all those appalling movies and appeared to be in freefall."

Jon looked down at his list of the remaining auditionees. There was only Olivia and Tom to come, followed by Katie Wilkes-Cox, and he knew all their work very well. In the case of Katie Wilkes-Cox rather too well, after his experiences with her on *The Sound of Music*. Alicia had told him that Olivia didn't want to be cast as anything major and Katie couldn't be, but he was wondering whether Tom might be a perfect Buttons. The age gap between him and Amber wouldn't matter so much; in fact, it would make the relationship all the more hopeless and touching.

"Livy? Tom? Are you there? I haven't got all night," shouted Jon impatiently.

"Coming!" came the muffled reply. There was a tinny tinkle of music and then suddenly a large pantomime horse appeared on stage. It had soft brown fur, massive brown eyes with thick lashes, a tail that swished magnificently and a daisy in the middle of its forehead. The children in the theatre shrieked, and the horse gave a loud whinny and galloped down the steps and into the auditorium. It tap-danced its way up the aisle, its front two feet perfectly coordinated and its back two tripping over each other. It cocked its head and pricked up its ears becomingly, flirted outrageously with the audience and Jon, and put out its head to be patted. Laughing, the children reached out to stroke it, and the horse whinnied with pleasure and fluttered its huge eyelashes. That brought the house down. The children were screaming with laughter as the music from *Swan Lake* started up and the horse started a lumbering dance.

Jon's face creased with laughter. "OK, Tom and Livy," he said. "That was fabulous. But there *is* no panto horse in Michael's script."

The horse dropped to its knees in front of Jon, put its front hooves together and begged, all the while batting its huge eyelashes and pretending to wipe away tears. Most of the Swans were doubled up with laughter and Jon held up his hands in surrender.

"All right, all right," he cried. "You win. I give in. You can be the panto horse. I'll ask Michael to write one in."

A noise that was a cross between a neigh and a cheer came from inside the horse, which rose to its feet, gave a little jig of joy and then collapsed in a heap on the floor. Then it scrambled up like a newborn foal and galloped off into the wings. Everyone cheered.

It took a few minutes for everyone to settle

down again after the excitement and Jon had to ask for quiet several times.

"OK," he said. "Katie, are you ready?"

Katie popped her head out from the wings. "Yes," she said, trying to sound bright and cheerful. "I'm ready."

"Then let's begin," said Jon.

The music struck up. Katie ran on the stage and started to sing "If I Were a Bell" from *Guys and Dolls*. She had got to the end of the verse and was singing "If I were a bell, I'd go ding dong, ding dong ding!" when Mrs Gibbs appeared at the door of the theatre, raised her hand to get Poppy Churchill, the accompanist and the Swan's head girl, to stop and said, "So very sorry, everyone, for interrupting, but I've got New York on the phone for you, Mr James. They say that they've been trying your mobile but it's off and it's really urgent. I told them you were auditioning but they said they had to speak with you without delay. They wouldn't take no for an answer."

Katie had faltered to a halt and stood looking uncomfortable. Mrs Gibbs glanced at her apologetically. "I'm really very sorry, Katie."

Jon ran his hands through his hair. "I'm sorry too, guys. I know it's unprofessional but I really do have to take this call. Forgive me, Katie, and stay exactly where you are. I'll be straight back and we can take it from the top." He followed Mrs Gibbs out of the door.

Katie stood on the stage on one leg, trying to look unconcerned. There was a moment's silence, then a few people began chatting and Poppy went over to chat to her friends. Suddenly a voice at the back of the theatre began singing very clearly, "If I were a smell I'd go ping pong, ping pong ping."

Some of the girls giggled; everyone else looked embarrassed and stopped chatting. Katie tried to pretend she hadn't heard a thing but gave herself away by turning bright red.

"Ping, pong, ping pong ping," trilled Kylie. "There *is* a nasty smell in here. Must be coming from the stage."

There was a charged silence. Poppy looked worried, as if she knew she ought to do something but wasn't sure what. A few girls laughed uncertainly; others looked unhappy, as if they thought Kylie had crossed a line. Katie looked wildly around as if seeking help, her eyes filled with tears, then she made a choking noise and stumbled off the stage.

Aeysha stood up very calmly from where she'd been sitting and walked down the auditorium until she was standing right in front of Kylie. Kylie stood up with her arms folded and a sulky, challenging look on her face. Aeysha leaned forward until her face was close to Kylie's and, making sure everyone could hear her, said, "What is your problem, Kylie Morris? One day, one day very, very soon, it will be you standing on a stage somewhere and I have no doubt that somebody will do to you what you have just done to Katie. As my mum always says, what goes around comes around." She smiled sweetly. "Do you know what you are, Kylie Morris? Because I do, and so does everybody else in this theatre today. You are nothing but a coward and a big bully."

Aeysha's grave voice carried a quiet authority. Kylie turned beetroot red; a number of her friends looked deeply embarrassed and shifted in their seats. There was another minute's pause and then somebody broke into applause and others followed, and some even cheered what Aeysha had said. Everyone was getting fed up with Kylie and she had gone too far this time. One of the unwritten rules of Swan auditions was that everybody was treated with courtesy and respect.

For a moment Kylie's eyes blazed. She looked around at her friends for support, but they all seemed to be mesmerised by their feet. For a moment it looked as if she might spit in Aeysha's face, but then she barged her way along the row and flounced out of the door, almost knocking over a surprised Jon James on his way back in. Not a single one of her friends followed her. Jon looked around at all the serious faces. He could feel the tension in the air.

"Is everything all right?" he asked, before turning to the stage. "Katie, my apologies. Are you ready? Katie!" He turned to the others, perplexed. "Where is she?"

"She felt a bit sick," said Aeysha.

Jon looked worried. He knew something must have happened but he wasn't a teacher; he had no idea what to do in these circumstances. Normally when he held children's auditions for professional productions he had a full back-up of staff to deal with this sort of thing. He was the director, not the babysitter.

"Is somebody looking after her?" he asked lamely.

"I was just about to go and see," said Aeysha.

"I'm coming too," said Georgia.

"Should I wait in case she comes back?"

"I don't think she'll be back," said Aeysha. "Not today, anyway."

"OK," said Jon with some relief. "Auditions over, kids."

Chapter Eleven

"It was awful," said Georgia. "But Aeysha was amazing to stand up to Kylie like that. She was awesome." She blushed. "She made the rest of us look like total cowards. Kylie looked as if she wanted to kill Aeysha but when she realised that she wasn't getting any support from her gang she just stomped out and none of them went after her."

"I wish I'd been there to see it," said Olivia.

"Where were you?" asked Georgia.

"Tom got stuck in the horse's head. I had to get Pablo to help me get him out. By the time we did he'd worked himself up into quite a state. He said he was going to die from heatstroke if he stayed in there a minute longer."

"Where did you get that amazing panto

horse costume?" asked Aeysha curiously. "It looks like a real antique."

"At an old music hall called Campion's Palace of Varieties. Tom and I found it in Hangman's Alley. We'll take you, if you like."

Georgia wrinkled her nose. "I don't like it around Hangman's Alley. It's too spooky. I always think I might come face to face with a ghost. In fact, I thought I saw one once, an old woman in an old-fashioned evening dress hobbling down the alley. I didn't stick around to find out where she went."

"Well, you don't have to come," said Olivia, smiling to herself. "Finish telling me about Katie. Is she OK?"

Aeysha and Georgia frowned. "We've looked everywhere, but we can't find her. We tried ringing her mobile too. She must be here somewhere because some of her stuff's still in the girls' cloakroom," said Georgia. "She was so upset when Kylie started singing. I thought she was going to dissolve into a puddle right there on the stage and disappear."

"I bet she wanted to," said Olivia. "But Georgia's right, Aeysha, you were brave to tackle Kylie. Do you think we should tell Gran what happened? I think she'd want to know."

Aeysha looked uncomfortable. "It would be too much like snitching."

"Maybe we should just wait and see if it all settles down?" said Georgia. "Now the others have seen Aeysha standing up to Kylie and humiliating her, with any luck they'll be less trouble. Without Kylie as a ringleader I reckon they'll give Katie-baiting a rest."

"I hope you're right," said Olivia. "I'm not sure Tom's so right about Katie being a survivor. I think with enough pressure she could break. Let's try and find her."

Katie sat hunched in the little cupboard in the girls' cloakroom. She rubbed the tears off her cheeks fiercely with the back of her hand and listened hard. Everyone else had long gone home and even Olivia and the others appeared to have given up looking for her. It was ages since she had heard them calling her name and the last thing she remembered was Georgia saying, "Well, maybe she did just go home without her things," and Olivia replying uncertainly, "Without her coat? Tell you what, I'll text her."

Katie looked at her tacky pay-as-you-go

mobile that she had on silent. She hadn't had a call or a text for a while. She decided that it must be safe to come out now. She would get her coat and bag and scoot off home and never come back. What was the point? Everybody hated her at the Swan. Nobody had stood up for her in the theatre. Not Georgia and Aeysha, not even Olivia and Tom, who must have been back in the auditorium by then. They had all stayed silent while Kylie Morris had sung that horrible, horrible song about her. They had just let her do it. She was sure they were only looking for her now because they felt guilty.

It just proved to Katie that she would never be accepted as a Swan. It had been a mistake to come back. She should have just gone to the local comp and given up on her dream of performing. Whatever hopes she had had of making a go of things at the school and of being accepted had been crushed by the last few weeks. She should let her dreams wither and perish, quit the dancing and acting and singing and just hunker down to harsh, grey reality. What was the point of trying to keep your dreams alive when other people just stamped all over them?

Katie felt overwhelmed by self-pity. Who

was she to think that she could make a comeback at the Swan? Tomorrow she'd do what her mum did, and just stay in bed. She doubted anyone at the Swan would really miss her. They might not even notice.

She scrambled out from the cupboard and collected her things. Peeping out of the door of the girls' cloakroom to check that the coast was clear, she scurried along the corridor as quiet as a mouse. Alicia's door was open and she could hear her talking to Mrs Gibbs. She paused. Before her panto audition she had vowed to confess to Miss Swan about putting her name on the Zelda audition list. But there was no point now. She wasn't ever coming back to the Swan.

She heard Alicia say, "So these are the Swan pupils that the *Zelda* production company wants to see?"

"Yes, I just got the email from Poppet. She wants you to ring her to confirm that they are all still available. Their first auditions will be the day after tomorrow."

Katie couldn't stop listening. Alicia was clearly scanning the list and thinking out loud.

"Aeysha, Georgia, Poppy, Anouska, Betty and Chloe, that's good. A pity about Nicola, she deserves her chance. I wonder if I can get them to reconsider. Can't say I'm heartbroken they don't want to see Kylie Morris; she's being such a little minx at the moment. Jon said he thought something went down at the panto auditions this afternoon but he didn't seem to know the details."

Katie was frozen outside the door, but her heart leapt to hear that Kylie wouldn't be getting a shot at Zelda. She knew it was mean, but after what had happened this afternoon she couldn't help but feel satisfied by the news. Kylie would be furious.

Alicia was saying some other names out loud. "Kate Carmichael? Who's she? Oh, there's a note here. They can't find her in Spotlight but they'll see her anyway. I'll tell Poppet when I ring her that she's not one of ours. She must be from some other school and Poppet has put her on our list by mistake."

Katie's brain was whirling. The *Zelda* people wanted to see her! Well, it had come too late! She crept past the open door. Fortunately Alicia and Mrs Gibbs were so engrossed in their conversation, they didn't notice her. She heard Alicia ask for Poppet's mobile number and Mrs

Gibbs reel it off for Alicia to scribble down. It was easy to remember, thought Katie; only a couple of digits different from her own number. She crept miserably out through the doors of the Swan and walked slowly down the steps. At the bottom she turned and looked back at the school. Tears ran down her face and she felt as if her heart were breaking.

"Goodbye," she whispered. "Goodbye forever."

Chapter Twelve

Georgia and Aeysha sat with the other Swan girls. They had already had their Zelda auditions and were waiting for the rest to finish so they could all set off back to the school together. It had been a very long morning. They saw Chloe leave the audition room and come over to join them. She pulled a face.

"They call that an audition? I didn't even get a chance to read."

"Me neither," said Betty. "I can't have been in there more than two minutes. They just looked me up and down and asked me a few questions."

"Stupid questions, if you ask me," said Chloe. "They wanted to know, if I was an animal, what animal would I be? I was tempted to say a very grumpy camel after sitting around here half the morning."

"They asked me what kind of flower I'd be," said Aeysha.

"They asked me that too," said Georgia eagerly. "What did you say?"

"I said I'd be a rambling rose because they're beautiful to look at and smell sweet but have wicked thorns if you get too close."

Georgia's face dropped. "Oh, Aeysha, that's so clever. I just said a daisy. I bet it was wrong."

"I don't think there's a wrong or a right answer, Georgie. I think they're just trying to get us to talk so they could get a feel for what we're like."

"I don't know why they didn't just let us read from the screenplay," said Anouska.

Aeysha waved an arm. "With all these girls to be seen? They'd be here for weeks if they let us all read for the part today. I guess they want to whittle us down first."

"I heard somebody say that they saw people all day yesterday and the day before too, and there's another lot this afternoon," said Nicola. "We don't stand a chance. It's like an open audition. We might just as well be auditioning for one of those TV reality shows."

"You know what will happen," said Betty gloomily. "The usual thing. They'll see hundreds of stage-school girls. Then they'll announce that they can't find anyone suitable and they want somebody completely fresh and untrained and launch a nationwide search in a blaze of publicity. We're wasting our time."

"Well, somebody's got to be lucky," said Georgia stubbornly. She hugged herself. Maybe this time it would be her. She just wished she hadn't said daisy. She really wished she'd said what Aeysha had said. She felt so envious of her friend.

"Liv! Slow down," said Tom. "We don't have to run all the way to Campion's."

Olivia swung round. Tom noticed how pale she was; her skin had a ghostly sheen. There were dark circles under her eyes as if she hadn't been sleeping well.

"I just want to get there. We don't have much time. We have to be back again for afternoon lessons and I promised Gran that we wouldn't be late. Come on. I want to check that

Ella and Arthur are all right."

Tom sighed. They had checked that Ella and Arthur were all right yesterday and the day before that. They were really grateful to the old people for lending them the fantastic panto horse costume though. When Alicia had seen it, her mouth dropped open with delight and surprise.

"You do realise you've been entrusted with something very precious and you must take real care of it?" she had told Olivia and Tom. They'd nodded, although Tom noted that Olivia hadn't explained the full extent of the treasure house that was Campion's. Alicia had given them money to buy a huge bouquet of flowers for Ella, and had sent them to deliver it with a handwritten invitation to the Swan panto. She had encouraged Olivia and Tom to keep visiting, telling them it was the least they could do. "I'm sure they don't get many visitors. Lots of old people get very lonely."

But Tom felt that Olivia was overdoing the visiting. She seemed to be obsessed by Campion's. She wanted to spend every spare minute there, walking the high-wire and talking to Ella and Arthur about the theatre and its history. When she was there, something about her changed. She was dreamier and more distant, as if she was hearing somebody far away talking to her in her head. Tom found it spooky. It was as if she was possessed. If it was up to him, he'd keep away from Campion's, but he felt he had to keep going with Olivia so he could keep an eye on her. He was concerned for his friend.

"Are you sure you're all right, Liv? You look completely exhausted."

"I'm fine, Tom. I'm just not sleeping so good." Olivia paused, and then she added, "I have this terrible nightmare almost every night. It's always the same. You know Henley Street, by the bridge?"

Tom nodded.

"Well, I'm walking there alone and I can hear a clock striking midnight, and when it gets to the last chime, there's a huge explosion like a bomb going off and then the bridge begins to fall down on top of me and I feel I'm going to suffocate, and that's when I always wake up."

Tom grimaced. "It sounds horrid."

"It is," said Olivia. "What do you think it means?" She sounded really anxious.

"It doesn't mean anything," said Tom. "It's just a dream." He grinned. "But to be on the safe side maybe you should avoid walking by the Henley Street bridge."

Ella had shown them the back entrance to Campion's and it was this that they always used. It led straight into the dimly lit auditorium with its shadowy nooks and crannies. Olivia was struck each time by the theatre's shabby, faded beauty. She glanced into one of the mottled mirrors and gasped. Instead of seeing herself and Tom reflected back, she thought she saw an image of two children dressed in the clothes from more than half a century before. She pointed speechlessly at the mirror.

Tom was puzzled. "What? It's only us, Liv. Anyone would think you'd just seen a ghost." He peered at her suspiciously. "You didn't think you *had* seen a ghost, did you?"

Olivia shook her head a little too quickly. "Just a trick of the light," she said casually, but Tom caught the quaver in her voice.

Arthur was alone in the theatre, sweeping the stage. He looked pleased to see the two children.

"Where's Ella?" asked Olivia.

"She's having a little nap," said Arthur. "She doesn't sleep well."

"Just like you, Liv," said Tom jokily.

"Oh, Ella has such terrible dreams," said Arthur sadly. "She dreams of clocks striking midnight, explosions and bridges falling. . ." He would have gone on but Olivia had made a choking sound and Tom's eyes had darkened and a look of horror had crossed his face.

Then they heard a noise behind them. It was Ella. She walked towards them as if she was sleepwalking and stretched out her arms as if to embrace them.

"Lizzie, Davey. You've come back. You've come back to forgive me. At last." Her tears began to fall, and then she drew back and her mood changed suddenly, just as it had the first time Olivia and Tom met her.

"You're not Lizzie and Davey! You're spies. *He's* sent you, hasn't he? Well," she drew herself up to her full height, "tell Prince from me that I know all about his tricks and schemes, and he'll never get his hands on Campion's. Never! Campion's will stay the way it has always been – forever!"

Chapter Thirteen

It was another hour before the Swans were finished at the Zelda auditions, and as they set off back to the Tube station, Aeysha checked her phone.

"I've got a text from Livy. Apparently Katie didn't turn up for school again today, and she still hasn't replied to any of our texts or calls," she said.

"Maybe she's not very well?" said Georgia.

"Possibly," said Aeysha. "But what if she's too upset to come back? I've been thinking about what happened. When Kylie started singing, none of us said anything. We were all too shocked. I couldn't really believe what I was hearing. It took me a few moments to react."

"Yes, but then you did say something,"

said Georgia.

Aeysha shrugged. "But Katie doesn't know that. She'd gone by then. From her point of view it would seem very much as if we all sat by and let Kylie get away with bullying her. Maybe she thinks we all secretly agreed with her? I'm going to talk to Livy. I think we should go to Katie's house, find out what's going on."

They stopped at some traffic lights at a busy road junction. Georgia peered into the window of a little café next to them. Through the half-steamed-up window she could see a girl with long, blonde and very straight hair sitting on her own at a table. From behind she looked just like Katie. The girl half turned and Georgia gave a little gasp. It *was* Katie! What was she doing there when she should be miles away at the Swan?

"Look!" hissed Georgia, suddenly nudging Aeysha. "I don't think Katie's sick."

Aeysha looked through the window. But the girl had turned round again and a man had sat down at the table behind her, obscuring the view.

"It's probably just someone who looks like her," said Aeysha as the lights changed and they started to cross the road. "There must be thousands of girls in London with long blonde hair."

Georgia glanced backwards. She had been certain it was Katie, but she must have been mistaken. But if it wasn't her, then there was somebody running around London who looked remarkably like her.

"Are you quite sure this is the right place?" said Aeysha doubtfully.

Olivia looked at the address she had scribbled down on a sheet of paper. She nodded. "Gran gave it to me when I said Katie wanted us to take some work round."

"Well," said Aeysha, "it's certainly a bit different from what she's used to."

The entrance to the flat was down an alley at the back of a row of mostly boarded-up shops. The alley was piled high with broken bags of rubbish, and as Olivia and Aeysha entered the alley something suspiciously like a rat scurried away.

"Ugh," said Aeysha. "To think Katie has to walk down here alone every day. Even when it's dark and she comes back late after extra classes at school. And it took us ages to get here."

Olivia looked at the peeling front door. "I think we can safely say that there's no luxury swimming pool or bathrooms with gold-plated taps behind there."

"Poor Katie," sighed Aeysha. "And that's something I never thought I'd say."

Olivia looked anxious. "Do you think Katie's going to mind that we've seen where she lives? She's got a lot of pride."

"Mmm, I hadn't thought of that," said Aeysha. "But if we just go away she might never come back to the Swan. It's been a week. We'll have to risk it."

"Mrs Gibbs told Gran that Mrs Wilkes-Cox had rung in to say she was ill. Maybe she really is sick."

"Sick at heart, more like," said Aeysha. "Look, we may be about to hurt Katie's pride and she may accuse us of sticking our noses in where we're not wanted, but if we do nothing, if we don't show her that we care about her and respect her, she may chuck the Swan in completely, and school could be all that's keeping her afloat. We have to try to talk to her."

"You're very persuasive, Aeysha. You

should be a lawyer or a hostage negotiator," said Olivia, and she lifted the knocker and let it fall. They waited but there was no answer.

Olivia knocked again. "They must be out," she said.

"I'm not so sure. I think I saw a curtain twitch upstairs," said Aeysha.

Olivia bent down, pushed open the letter box and peered through. All she could see were uncarpeted stairs.

"Try shouting," said Aeysha.

"Katie!" called Olivia. "Katie, it's Livy and Aeysha. Please answer the door. We want to talk to you. We're really missing you at the Swan."

They waited a moment. There was no sound or movement from inside the flat. Olivia straightened up. "We're wasting our time. There's nobody here."

Aeysha bent to the letter box and shouted through it. "Katie! Katie, please open the door. We've got things we need to say to you."

Silence.

"Let's go," said Olivia. They'd started to walk down the little alley when they heard the sound of the front door being opened. They turned back expectantly, but it was not Katie but her mum who stood there, her head peering out of the half-open door. Her hair looked unwashed and she was clutching her dressing gown closed at the neck.

"I thought it might be the bailiffs again, which was why I didn't answer," she said apologetically. "But then I realised it was Katie's friends." She tried to smile brightly, and Olivia was reminded of a little bird with a damaged wing she had once seen who was still singing cheerfully despite its injury.

"Hello, Mrs Wilkes-Cox," said Aeysha. "This is Livy and I'm Aeysha."

Mrs Wilkes-Cox smiled. "I remember you, Aeysha. You used to come to Katie's swimming-pool parties. . ." Her voice trailed off.

"We came to see Katie," said Olivia. "Is she in?"

Mrs Wilkes-Cox looked puzzled. "No, she's still at school. She has an extra dance class on Thursday."

"But," Olivia blurted out, "Katie wasn't at school today."

Mrs Wilkes-Cox gasped. "But she left this morning as usual. We must call the police! Something terrible must have happened to her."

Aeysha shook her head and frowned at Olivia. They were really not handling this very well. "I don't think so, Mrs Wilkes-Cox," she said gently. "You see, she hasn't been at school all week."

Mrs Wilkes-Cox frowned. "But she's got up and gone out at the same time as normal every morning."

"So," asked Olivia, "you didn't ring school to say she was sick?"

"No," said Mrs Wilkes-Cox helplessly. "I thought she was going to the Swan. It's been the one good thing in her life, something to hang on to when everything else – including me – has been so rubbish."

"She was coming. Every single day until the auditions last week."

Mrs Wilkes-Cox scrutinised their faces. "Did something happen at the auditions?" she asked sharply. She pulled open the door. "I think you'd better come in and tell me all about it."

Chapter Fourteen

Katie walked slowly down the street. She was shivering and for once she would be glad to get home, if you could call it home. But even the bare, unwelcoming flat was better than being out on the streets all day. The last week had been awful. She hadn't dared tell her mum that she wouldn't be going back to the Swan. She didn't want her mum to know: she was depressed enough as it was without having to worry about Katie too. Katie wanted to protect her, and if she explained how Kylie had treated her and how nobody had bothered to stand up to her she would have to admit to her mum how much she felt that she had deserved what had happened to her because of her own behaviour in the past. Which was why she had just got up every morning as usual, put on her uniform and left the house at the same time as if she was heading off to school.

Katie wished that you could just shed your past life like a snake could shed its skin. But it wasn't so easy. She'd only ever be able to reinvent herself if they moved somewhere far away where nobody knew them. How she longed to be able to start all over again, like getting a new blank exercise book at the start of the school year.

Apart from going to the Zelda audition, she'd spent the last week riding the Circle line on the Tube, sitting on the top of buses and hanging out in parks and shopping centres, where she went into the lavatories to change out of her school uniform. She'd thought the week was never going to end. She was cold a great deal of the time and she didn't dare stay in one place too long in case she attracted attention. In one shopping centre the security guards had asked her why she wasn't at school and it was only because of her acting skills that she managed to persuade them that she was old enough to have left already.

She jumped as her phone rang. She

expected it to be Aeysha or Olivia or Georgia or even Tom. They had all tried ringing her on and off, and left messages. She wished they would stop. It was only guilt or, even worse, pity that was making them ring. She looked at the number, and her heart lurched. It was Poppet from Kylight Productions. She pressed answer as she turned into the alley, her nose wrinkling at the rank smell of decay.

"Hello, Kate speaking."

"Kate, sweetie. It's Poppet. Good news! The casting agents have put you forward. The director wants to hear you read. Tomorrow, two p.m. I'll text you the office address. Is that all right?"

"Yes," whispered Katie, who was standing quite still with the shock of the news.

"You're a very lucky girl, Kate Carmichael. You're in with a real chance to play Zelda," said Poppet chirpily. "There are girls all over the country wishing they were standing in your shoes."

"Yes," said Katie, looking down at where her foot was resting on a greasy Chinese takeaway carton. "I expect there are." She said goodbye to Poppet and headed for the front door. She put her key in the lock, turned and pushed the door open to find her mum, Olivia and Aeysha all looking expectantly at her.

Her mum got to her feet. "Oh, Katie," she said tearfully. "Where have you been? I've been so worried about you. Where have you been going every day? Your friends say you haven't been at the Swan all week."

Katie stared furiously at Olivia and Aeysha. Her friends were looking anxious and embarrassed, hoping she'd know they hadn't meant to get her into trouble.

Katie looked back at them unsmilingly. "What friends?" she said. "I certainly haven't got any at the Swan. Those that don't hate me just pity me." She made a choking noise. "I'm never going back. If there's one thing I've learned over the last few weeks it's that I can't rely on anyone. Not on you, Mum, and definitely not on my so-called friends. I'm just going to make it on my own." She burst into heart-rending sobs, but when her mum and Olivia and Aeysha rushed to hug her she pushed them all away.

On the bus on the way home, Olivia and Aeysha were very quiet. They were shocked by Katie's circumstances and her evident despair. After a long silence Olivia said quietly, "Do you think it counts as snitching if you tell somebody something about somebody else that they really ought to hear and that they might be able to help make better, even if it got somebody else into really big trouble?"

Aeysha found Olivia's hand and squeezed it. "No," she said. "I don't think it would count as snitching at all."

Chapter Fifteen

Aeysha and Georgia had grown very curious about Olivia and Tom's frequent disappearances and eventually they forced their friends to tell them where they'd been going. Olivia and Tom swore Aeysha and Georgia to secrecy, as they didn't want lots of Swans turning up unexpectedly in Hangman's Alley. Aeysha and Georgia had been wide-eyed when Olivia described Campions magical interior.

"It's just like the enchanted castle in *Sleeping Beauty*," she enthused, "only it's a theatre. The most magical theatre in the whole world."

Tom stayed strangely quiet. Aeysha, perceptive as ever, had noticed, and afterwards, when Olivia had slipped away and Georgia had mysteriously said she had to dash too, she had asked him why he didn't share Olivia's enthusiasm.

Tom spoke hesitantly. "Liv's right. Campion's *is* beautiful, in a faded, rickety kind of way. But it's also quite weird and it's making Liv weird too. Ella doesn't help. One minute she's delighted to see us but clearly thinks we're some other kids called Davey and Lizzie, and the next she behaves as if we are spies sent by someone who wants to take Campion's away from her. I actually find it all really creepy, but Liv is completely obsessed with the place. She wants to go there all the time. It's as if she's being drawn to it by an invisible force, or ghost or something."

"You mean the theatre's haunted?" asked Aeysha, shivering.

"I don't know," said Tom. "But I think Olivia hears things and maybe even sees things when we're there, and she's been having the weirdest dreams and is so pale sometimes she looks like a ghost herself."

"But she seems pretty normal to me," said Aeysha. "And she's always a bit distracted and pale!"

Tom nodded. "I know. And when she's here, she's like the same old Liv. But you should see her at Campion's or when we get near to the place. It's as if she's possessed. It's so weird."

Aeysha sighed. "She's not the only one behaving weirdly. Georgia is being really odd too. Yesterday she actually said that she thought maybe we shouldn't see so much of each other while we were both still up for the Zelda role, and this morning she didn't come and sit next to me on the bus like she normally does but went and sat on her own."

"That is seriously bonkers behaviour," agreed Tom, "but not half as weird as Liv's."

He was about to admit that he was frightened when Olivia appeared, holding her coat.

"Come on, Tom, hurry up. Campion's is waiting for us," she said. "I can feel it."

Tom and Aeysha pulled a face at each other, but Olivia was too concerned with hurrying Tom away to notice. As they were leaving, Aeysha called after Tom, "Why don't you have a poke around on the Web, Tom? You never know, you might come up with something that explains everything."

"What was Aeysha talking about?" asked Olivia curiously as they headed towards Hangman's Alley.

"Eh, nothing," said Tom. "It was just about my history project."

"Oh," said Olivia, losing interest and forgetting that they didn't even have history projects. She just glided along the pavement towards Campion's like someone being pulled by an invisible thread. She looked so strange, it made Tom come out in goosebumps.

A few days later, Olivia and Tom jumped off the high-wire on the stage at Campion's. Olivia grinned at Ella and gave a mock curtsy. The little ghost-light was still flickering in its jam jar but had been moved to the side of the stage. Olivia ran to fetch it and placed it back centre stage.

"Good, we must always appease the ghosts and keep them happy," said Ella approvingly. "Now it's time for tea."

It was clearly one of Ella's better days. Olivia felt relieved and glanced at Tom. It had been quite a struggle to get him to keep coming after they had discovered that Ella's dreams were spookily like the nightmares that Olivia was having. Olivia had refused point blank to discuss it. She was just glad he was here today.

Tom looked at Olivia's pale face and resolved to look Campion's up on the Internet that evening. He was cross with himself for being too busy to do it before. Once he had, maybe he should speak to Alicia. But what would he say? That he thought Campion's was haunted and that Olivia was seeing ghosts? And this to a woman who had made it quite clear that she didn't believe in such superstitious nonsense.

Besides, Alicia was preoccupied with preparations for the pantomime. She was spending a lot of the time on the phone to Theo's and Amber's agent, Sheridan, trying to negotiate rehearsal times. Then a crisis had blown up only that morning when the stage designer announced she'd got a last-minute job in New York and wouldn't be able to work on *Cinderella* as she'd promised. Alicia was being stoic about it, saying that if you asked people to work for free, even if it was for a good cause, it wasn't surprising if you didn't get their full commitment, but all the Swans could see that she had her hands full with the production.

"Make yourselves at home," said Ella as

she handed around the tea cups.

"It does feel like home," said Olivia happily.

Ella put down her tea cup and said, "Does it really, Livy dear?"

Olivia nodded.

"It's so lovely to hear the sound of children laughing again in the theatre," said Ella. "It has been such a long time," she added wistfully.

"But I always hear children laughing when I'm in the theatre; I heard them just now when we were on the wire," blurted Olivia. She stopped and reddened. Tom was looking at her as if she was mad, but Ella suddenly looked alert and interested like a small, beady-eyed bird.

"Do you have children, Ella?" asked Olivia, suddenly curious.

Ella shook her head sadly. "I never married," she said. "I was married to Campion's instead." Her eyes glazed over as she was caught in the web of her own thoughts. "Once I did think my prince had come, but I was deceived. It wasn't love, it was just greed. I've never known true love."

Olivia saw Arthur gazing at Ella, and noticed him flinch when she said that she had never known love. It came to her in a flash: Arthur loved Ella. It was why he had stayed with her all these years, long after Campion's had closed down. His love had gone unrequited all that time. It made her think of poor Buttons in *Cinderella,* who was devoted to a girl who never saw him as anything but her best friend. Olivia's heart contracted.

Then Tom broke the spell. "Actually, why did Campion's close?" he asked. "You've never said. There must have been a reason."

As soon as the words were out of his mouth, he regretted them. Arthur frowned at him, and Ella seemed to grow frailer than ever and left the table abruptly.

"I'm sorry," said Tom quickly. "I didn't mean to upset her. I just don't understand why there's so much mystery. I feel like I'm trying to solve a riddle without all the clues."

"That's all right, lad," said Arthur kindly. "You two coming here has brought back the past to Ella. She keeps trying to push it away when what she really needs to do is exorcise it, but that's never going to happen while she continues to keep the theatre as a shrine. She won't stop punishing herself. I've been hoping that you might be the two to help her and Campion's, given what happened and all."

Tom and Olivia were puzzled. They didn't really understand what Arthur was talking about or how they could help, and all the talk of exorcism was making Tom feel spooked again.

"Did something bad happen here? Something to do with children?" he asked anxiously. Arthur looked as if he was about to speak, but at that moment Ella returned to the table as if nothing had happened and said brightly, "Would anyone like another cup of tea?"

Tom and Olivia looked at each other. "Thank you but no," said Tom. "We've got to get back to the Swan by six o'clock. That's when the panto horse is being called for rehearsal."

"I'm so looking forward to seeing your routine," said Ella.

"We'd never have been able to do it if you hadn't lent us the costume," said Tom. "It's mint."

Olivia suddenly looked thoughtful. "I wonder if it's possible to do a panto horse routine on the high-wire. I wonder if anyone has ever tried it. . ."

"Count me out," laughed Tom. "I find trying to control my own two feet on the wire hard enough; dealing with four would be terrifying."

"We should at least give it a try," said Olivia with a grin. "Who knows, with a bit of hoofing around we may do it."

They were still arguing about it good-humouredly as they said goodbye and made their way down into Hangman's Alley. Tom was pleased to see Olivia behaving more like her normal self. But it didn't last. As they left, Olivia looked up at the Campion's window that overlooked the alley and suddenly froze. Her face went blank and her eyes were glassy. She leaned forward. She could see two children standing looking down at her and Tom, their noses pressed against the glass. They were smiling at her and beckoning. Her head started to fill with children's whispers and giggles, and she could hear what they were saying very clearly: *"Livy, Livy. You can't catch us!"*

"What do you want?" she said out loud.

"Liv! Liv!" Tom's voice sounded really scared. "Liv, what is it? What have you seen? Who are you talking to?"

Olivia shook herself. She looked up at the window. There was nobody there. She saw Tom's anxious face, smiled and said softly, "There's nothing to be afraid of, Tom. Everything's going to be all right."

Chapter Sixteen

Alicia sat opposite Katie's mum on one of the only two chairs in the poky maisonette. Alicia smiled gently. "It's so good of you to allow me to come and see you, Mrs Wilkes-Cox. I know things have been hard for you. I'm very grateful for your time."

"It's Katie. . ." began Mrs Wilkes-Cox doubtfully. "She's. . . she's. . ." She tailed off miserably.

"She's a very talented girl," said Alicia firmly, "but possibly not the happiest of children just at this moment. She was so brave to expose her father's criminal activities. I know she used to hero-worship him. The change of circumstances must be very difficult for her, and you."

Mrs Wilkes-Cox blushed.

"I'm glad she's back in school again," continued Alicia. "Thank you for notifying us about her absence. It must be very hard for her to settle at the Swan after everything that has happened. And of course, some of the children are unforgiving. But I assure you, Mrs Wilkes-Cox, that I do know what is going on and I am dealing with those who need dealing with. They are not bad girls, just thoughtless, self-obsessed and in need of taking down a peg or two. I'd be very surprised if there are any further incidents. I don't think you need have any worries on that score, and if you do you should of course contact me immediately. We must work together to ensure Katie's future. I have such faith in Katie and I want her to get the chance to blossom and fulfil her potential."

"Oh," said Mrs Wilkes-Cox, at a loss for words. She felt as if Alicia was talking in some kind of code that she couldn't quite decipher, and the meaning was under the words, not in the words themselves. "Oh, I. . ."

Alicia waited a moment but when it became apparent that Mrs Wilkes-Cox was not going to say anything further, she continued,

"But I didn't just want to talk about Katie, Mrs Wilkes-Cox. I need to talk about you."

"Me?!" The other woman's heart sank. She was certain that Alicia was about to say that she was an unfit mother, that she had let her daughter down utterly, and that now Alicia had no choice but to alert social services. Katie might even be taken into care!

"Yes, you, Mrs Wilkes-Cox." Alicia smiled. "Some time ago Katie told Olivia that you were a stage designer before you married, and when Olivia heard that I was in urgent need of one for our pantomime, she remembered and mentioned it to me. I was wondering if you could help me out. It's not a properly paid job, I'm afraid, as the panto is for charity, but we can offer expenses and a small fee and it will be an excellent showcase for your talents. I can guarantee that lots of industry people will see your work.

"Please think about it, Mrs Wilkes-Cox," continued Alicia. "You would be doing me an enormous favour. The Swan would be very much in your debt."

Katie's mum felt like a drowning woman who had been thrown a lifeline. She had always loved her job as a stage designer and only reluctantly gave it up when she became pregnant with Katie. She had always regretted it.

"I don't know what to say," she said, and her eyes were moist.

"Well, just say yes then!" said Alicia. "I know you can do this." There was a little pause, then Alicia added softly, "Katie needs you, Mrs Wilkes-Cox, and the Swan needs you too."

"Thank you," said Katie's mum, her eyes shining. "Things have been bad, very bad, but maybe our luck is turning. This is just what I need." She added shyly, "I accept your offer. But I'd like it if you called me by my maiden name. Lily Wilkes-Cox is no more; I'm Lily Carmichael from now on."

"Lily Carmichael!" exclaimed Alicia. "But I know your work. You won an Olivier for your *Much Ado About Nothing* set in nineteenth-century India."

Lily nodded.

"Oh, that's amazing! We are privileged to have you," said Alicia. She took a quick look at her watch. "I'm afraid I must go. I have an appointment with some parents back at school and I have a taxi waiting."

* * *

Alicia leaned back in the taxi as it headed for the Swan. Lily Carmichael! It was quite a coup for the school, and she hoped it would be exactly what both Katie and her mum needed. She frowned. *Carmichael*. She knew she'd heard that name somewhere else recently. But for the life of her she couldn't remember where.

Chapter Seventeen

Georgia leaned forward, looked around to check that nobody else was listening and whispered, "Will Todd saw Kylie with her parents in the waiting room. Apparently Kylie's face was all blotchy as if she had been crying. Somebody must have snitched."

Olivia started tearing the piece of paper in front of her into tiny pieces.

"Whoever did it, did the right thing. I don't feel sorry for Kylie," said Aeysha smoothly. "I'm glad Miss Swan got to hear what happened and came down heavily on her. Maybe everyone will give Katie a break now. She's looked so down since she came back to school. I sat next to her at lunch, but for all the response I got, it was like trying to hold a conversation with a block of stone."

"I can understand why she wants to keep her distance," said Olivia, thinking about her own miserable first term at the Swan when she'd thought most people hated her. "It's hard to know how to be a good friend to her."

"We're so lucky we all have each other," said Aeysha. She turned to Georgia. "Do you want to go over the *Zelda* script together?" she asked.

"Hey, I forgot. The next audition's tomorrow, isn't it?" said Olivia. "Will that be the third time they've seen you both?"

"Fourth," said Aeysha. "Poppet said that if we get through this one, it will probably be a screen test next."

Georgia looked annoyed. "How do you know that? When were you talking to Poppet and why is she giving you special treatment?"

Aeysha frowned. "She's not giving me special treatment! I just asked her when she rang to confirm tomorrow's audition. Don't get upset, Georgia; she'd have told you if you'd asked."

"I just think everyone who has a chance at Zelda should be treated the same. It's not fair if some people know more than others. It puts them at an advantage." Georgia knew as she said it that she sounded silly and unreasonable. It was just that she so wanted to play Zelda and she was hungry for any titbit of information that might help her win the part.

Aeysha shrugged. "Well, now you know too. But I don't see how it puts either of us at an advantage. If I'd realised it was so important to you, I'd have told you as soon as Poppet told me. I'd always share anything I found out with you, Georgia, because you're my friend."

Georgia blushed furiously. "Sorry, Aeysha, I'm just a bit wound up over the audition."

"So shall we practise together and give each other a few tips?"

Georgia hesitated. "Actually, I think I'm a bit tired. It's been a long day."

Aeysha looked surprised and a little hurt. "Never mind," she said brightly, and quickly changed the subject. "Hey, have you heard Kasha's single yet? It's out and it's really good. Do you want to hear it? I've got a download on my phone."

* * *

Katie put her key in the door and sniffed. She could smell rosemary and thyme. The maisonette was full of the unfamiliar and quite delicious smell of a casserole cooking. She frowned. What on earth was going on? Who was cooking in their flat? She dropped her things by the door and walked through to the poky kitchen. Her mother was standing at the cooker with her back to her. She was fully dressed, and her hair was brushed and tied in a ponytail. The radio was tuned to a pop station, and her mum was humming as she stirred the casserole.

"Mum?" she said hesitantly.

Her mother spun round. She held out her arms. "Katie darling."

Katie stared closely at her face. She was wearing lipstick and her eyes were sparkling, not dull and full of misery as they usually were. It was months since she had seen her mum looking so well.

"What's going on?" she asked suspiciously.

Her mother's eyes filled with tears but she was smiling. "Katie. It's all going to be all right. I've been offered a job. It's not well paid. In fact, it's barely paid at all, just expenses and a bit on top. But it's a start. A new beginning. I feel as if I've woken up from a bad dream."

"That's great, Mum!" said Katie. "But how—"

"I had a visitor. Well, actually first of all I had a phone call. Then I had a visitor. Miss Swan."

Katie's heart began to thump. Why had Miss Swan come here? Had she discovered that Katie had been going to the Zelda auditions? Surely her mum wouldn't be smiling if that were the case. She couldn't bear to think Miss Swan had been here and seen where she lived. It was too, too horrible.

Her mother saw her stricken face. "Katie, listen to me. I know it's not nice to think of Miss Swan knowing our circumstances. But it's for the best. Oh, love, I've let you down so badly. I'm sorry. But it's time for me to be a parent again."

"What kind of job did she offer you?" asked Katie.

Her mother laughed out loud. "I'm going to design the Swan panto."

Katie gasped. "But that's amazing!"

"It's like a dream come true. And I'm

going back to my maiden name. Miss Swan recognised it and I hope others will too. It's a new beginning for both of us, Katie. We can put the past behind us and look to making a proper future." She enveloped Katie in her arms. "We're not going under, Katie; we're going to be OK. I can feel it in my bones."

Katie felt tears well in her eyes as she hugged her mother back. It was such a relief not to have to be the one holding it all together any more. She was so tired, so tired of everything. She wanted to let her mother look after her like she had when she was a little girl. She knew now she had to confess about the Zelda auditions, explain why she had done it and get her mum to help her make it all right.

"Mum," she said hesitantly, "I've got something I need to say. . ."

"What is it, darling?" asked her mum, looking into Katie's face. Katie saw shining eyes, her face suffused with the soft glow of hope, and knew she couldn't destroy the moment. She kissed her mother on the cheek.

"It's nothing, Mum. It doesn't matter." She sniffed. "Something smells great. Can we eat? I'm starving."

* * *

Tom clicked on the page and scrolled down. He had been so engrossed in what he was reading that he hadn't noticed the light had faded from the classroom. The computer screen cast an eerie glow on his pale, freckled face. He studied the page. It didn't add much to the history of Campion's that he didn't already know.

Ella had told him and Olivia that many famous music hall stars of the nineteenth and early twentieth centuries had performed there, ones with great names like Burlington Bertie and Marie Lloyd. She'd also told them about the famous dancer who had a bath in her dressing room and how the Stage Door Johnnies, with more money than sense, had queued to pay for it to be filled with pink champagne. The dancer loved to bathe in the bubbles.

There was also the chorus girl whose dress had caught on one of the naked flames on the stage and who would have burned to death but for the quick-thinking stage manager who threw a bucket of water over her and wrapped her in a Turkish rug. After that, she always danced wearing a veil to hide her scarred face, but it only added to her mysterious allure. One of her admirers had bought her a baby tiger that she kept in her dressing room until it escaped one night. It was never seen again, although for years afterwards there were reports of sightings of a full-grown tiger stalking the streets of Borough and Bermondsey.

There were the teenage twins everyone thought were boys, but who turned out to be the cross-dressing runaway daughters of a general, and the Chinese conjuror who was accidently shot doing his infamous catching-a-bullet-in-his-teeth trick, and who on his deathbed was revealed not to be Chinese at all, but the son of a Wapping cobbler.

Ella and Arthur had also shown Tom and Olivia the ancient stage machinery and the hidden trapdoors that were used in pantomime transformation scenes, when the characters or scenery changed dramatically with lots of smoke and music and gasps of amazement from the audience. Ella herself had played Cinderella on this very stage, and some of the backcloths from the production still existed, though they were very faded. But they were still beautiful; a piece of living theatre history.

"It's amazing; it should all be in a museum," Tom had said wonderingly, but Olivia shook her head firmly and said, "No, it belongs in a theatre."

Then a look of puzzlement crept into her eyes and she turned to Ella. "But I still don't understand why you don't use it. If it's not used, it might just as well be in a museum. It's dead, mummified. . ."

She would have gone on but she saw Arthur frowning at her, and Ella said sternly, "I made a vow and I will never break it. The theatre will remain permanently closed. No public performances." She looked sad, but determined. "At Campion's, the show will never go on again."

In the classroom, Tom sighed and clicked on another page. He didn't really know what he was looking for but he knew there was some mystery about Campion's and, as Ella and Arthur were reluctant to share whatever it was, he was determined to find out on his own. Perhaps if he knew what it was he wouldn't feel as spooked all the time. As he scanned the page, the door to the classroom opened and Olivia appeared.

"So this is where you've been hiding, Tom McCavity! I've been looking for you everywhere. I even tried texting you but I guess your phone must be on silent. I thought we were going to Campion's to try walking the high-wire as the panto horse." She paused. "Are you feeling all right? You look terrible. Is something wrong?"

Tom pointed silently at the computer screen. Olivia quickly glanced at it. She shrugged. "Why are you reading about an unexploded World War Two bomb? Oh, that's sad – it went off in 1951 and killed a woman and two children." She looked up at Tom.

"I can see it's a terrible tragedy, Tom, but I don't see why you're so upset. It all happened a very long time ago."

"Look at their names," whispered Tom.

Olivia looked further down the page and started reading. "'The deceased were Helen Campion, aged thirty-five and—'"

Tom finished the sentence for her. "'—her twins, Elisabeth and David Campion, aged eleven.' And look where it happened! Underneath the railway bridge in Henley Street at around midnight on Hallowe'en. Don't you see, Olivia? It all fits. They must be the children that Ella talks about all the time, the ones she keeps mistaking us for. And the dream you keep having, about the explosion and the bridge falling down, it's about them, it's their deaths."

Tom was sheet-white and shaking violently. "Promise me, Liv. You must never go back to Campion's. There's something sinister going on. We're being drawn into some kind of trap. If you won't promise me, I'm going to tell your gran and make her stop you."

Olivia looked shaken but her eyes blazed. "If you do that, Tom McCavity, I'll never speak to you again as long as I live. Anyway, it's a waste of time telling Gran. She doesn't believe in ghosts."

"So you agree that's what we're dealing with?" whispered Tom. "Ghosts?"

Olivia bit her lip. "I know you're worried, Tom. I know you think I might need help. But I don't. Yes, I dream things that can't be explained. I hear children and, yes, I see them too. But they don't frighten me. It's like being in a room and noticing that there are other people there who you've just not noticed before. Or it's like when you try and tune the radio to the station you want and you get interference and it sounds all crackly and strange. When I'm near Campion's, it feels as if I'm on a different wavelength. But it's not scary, it's quite exhilarating, and there's nothing sinister about it. I'm quite certain about that. If what I'm experiencing is ghosts, then I think I need to find out what they want and what they need from me. I don't need help, Tom. They do."

Chapter Eighteen

The music built to a crescendo and the cast struck a final pose. There was a drum roll and everyone stamped their feet in unison. As they did so, paint flaked off from the ceiling above the stage and dropped on to their heads. It looked as if the entire cast had suddenly developed a bad case of dandruff.

Eel, who was standing next to Theo in the wings, giggled. "Maybe this is going to be the first *Cinderella* ever to feature zombies," she said. Theo grinned at her. He liked Eel Marvell. He had met her on the first night of *The Sound of Music* and had been very impressed by her performance when she had suddenly been whisked out of the audience by Jon and on to the stage to play Gretl. She was a talented kid.

"Thank you, Swans, that was fantastic," said Jon. "Just a few notes." He looked at Poppy, who was stage-managing the show. "Any news on Amber?"

"On her way, apparently. Sheridan called. Amber had to go and see a specialist about her throat."

Jon made a face. "That doesn't sound good." He sighed. Rehearsing Theo and Amber was turning into a nightmare. There was such pressure on their time. Either they both didn't turn up and there would be lengthy explanations about sudden TV interviews or meetings about future jobs or, like today, one had turned up and not the other. Theo had already been here for over an hour, but there wasn't much that Jon could do with him without Amber. Fortunately, Theo seemed delighted to be reliving his school days, and Eel Marvell was keeping him entertained.

Jon began giving the chorus of villagers some notes on their song and dance. "That was great, Kylie, but remember to move upstage a little after you've got the water from the well. But it's coming along very nicely. I like what you're doing."

Kylie glowed in his praise. She had been

keeping her head down and working really hard since Miss Swan had called her and her parents in for that awful interview. It had been made crystal clear to Kylie that she was jeopardising her future at the Swan by her behaviour. She glanced towards the back of the theatre. Some of the rows of seats had been removed and a few of the children were helping Katie's mum paint the huge backcloth for the show.

Kylie blushed. She found she could never quite meet Katie's mum's eye. She had been invited on holiday with the Wilkes-Coxes in their more affluent days, and she had repaid Katie by bullying her. She couldn't quite believe how horrible she had been to Katie. She didn't even really know why she had done it, except to look big in the eyes of the other girls and to show Katie that she was top dog now. But instead she had been the one who had been made to look small. She felt really ashamed of herself. She wanted to say something to Katie, to tell her that she was sorry and she had been a cow, but she didn't dare approach her. However, she knew she had to do something to make reparation. She would ask some of her friends what she should do.

At that moment Katie looked up from her painting and saw Kylie looking at her. Katie's stomach lurched. Olivia and the others thought that Kylie had learned her lesson, but Katie wasn't sure they were right. What if Kylie was just biding her time? She looked away quickly. The memory of how Kylie had humiliated her still made her cheeks burn. Despite everything Miss Swan had said to her, and despite Olivia and her friends' support, Katie found it hard to put what had happened at the audition behind her. Every time she walked down a corridor she was acutely aware of the other pupils and was convinced that they were laughing at her behind her back.

Jon finished giving notes. He glanced at his watch again and wished Amber would hurry up. A small circle had gathered round Theo and they were cheering and whooping. Theo appeared to be having a tap-dancing competition with Eel and Will Todd, and from what Jon could see Theo was enjoying every moment of being soundly beaten.

"We won! We won!" shrieked Eel delightedly.

"I'm way out of practice," said Theo, who

was extremely breathless. "It's years since I did any serious dancing. I do love it so. I'd love to tap dance on a stage again. Except for *Hamlet* and *Henry V*, most princes are charming but really rather dull. But, Eel and Will, you won fairly and squarely and you deserve a prize. What would you like?"

Eel's eyes brightened. "Well, I've been trying to organise a trip to Somerset House for us all to go ice skating. But most people say it's too expensive and they can't afford it."

Olivia looked embarrassed. "Eel, I don't think Theo meant something massive like that," she said quickly. "It's too much." She turned to Theo. "I'm sorry, she's not normally so grasping, honest."

Theo grinned. "No, I think she's right, and besides, all you Swans deserve a treat. I'll get my PA to arrange it for everyone involved in *Cinderella*. My treat. Maybe once the panto previews are over and before the first night."

A great cheer went up and Eel squealed and flung her arms round Theo. "I could give you a few free tap-dancing lessons in return, if you like. I think you've got some talent. You would be quite good if you practised."

Olivia couldn't believe the cheek of her little sister but Theo just grinned. "I might take you up on that, Eel."

At that moment Amber Lavelle sailed into the theatre, dropping her fake fur coat the arms of the PA trailing behind her. She was wearing a tight leather catsuit and she had a crimson scarf wrapped around her throat that matched the gash of red lipstick on her mouth.

"How's the voice, Amber?" asked Jon sympathetically.

"Dreadful. Absolutely dreadful. I can barely whisper. And to make things worse, Kasha Kasparian has knocked me off the number-one spot in the singles' chart. I'm prepared to forgive him, though, because he's really rather cute. Oh, sometimes I think I'll just chuck it all in. . ." She paused as if expecting a storm of protest, and when it didn't come she added brightly, "But of course my fans would never let me. They'd be devastated."

Jon muttered sympathetically. "Amber darling, do you think you could manage a little rehearsal? Theo has been waiting for ages."

"Of course, Jon, but no singing. My doctor says I must rest my voice. I'll just go and touch up my make-up." And she sashayed off jabbering very loudly to someone on her mobile. She appeared to have forgotten all about resting her throat.

"Diva," whispered Eel, just loudly enough for those around her to hear.

"I didn't hear that, Eel," said Jon, and although his voice was sharp there was a twinkle in his eye.

Chapter Nineteen

Georgia finished reading the speech and waited. The director whispered something to the man next to him, who then whispered something to the woman next to him. Georgia strained to hear what they were saying.

"I don't know," said the woman, appraising Georgia with her grey eyes as if she was thinking of putting a bid in for her at an auction but wasn't sure she was worth the money. "She might work, but I suppose that depends on who you cast as Zelda's friend, Trinity. We don't want two blondes. That would never do."

"Maybe we could dye her hair," said the director, as if Georgia wasn't standing there right in front of him. She was beginning to feel quite angry, but she bit her lip and said nothing. The woman rifled through the photos on her desk.

"Of course, Aeysha's already dark; you wouldn't have to dye her hair."

Georgia froze. There was no way Aeysha was going to get the role just because she wasn't blonde. "I'd be happy to dye my hair," she blurted out. In fact, what she wanted to say was that she would dye her hair purple, cut off her right arm or donate a kidney if that's what it would take to get the role. But of course she didn't.

"Maybe we do want a blonde?" mused the director. He looked bored. "Or maybe we don't. Decisions. Decisions." He suddenly brightened. "I know – we need a redhead."

"Actually," said Poppet nervously, "you weeded out all the redheads at the first-look stage. You said you were certain that Zelda wasn't a redhead."

"Oh, did I?" said the director absently. He scrutinised Georgia again for what felt like hours. "Thank you, Georgina," he said eventually. "We'll let you know."

"Georgia," said Georgia vehemently. "It's

not Georgina, it's Georgia."

The director smiled weakly. "Of course, of course. Georgia. I knew that."

Georgia glared at him, enraged. They had called her back again and again, made her jump through hoop after hoop like a performing seal and they didn't even know her name.

"Well, you don't behave as if you do," she said furiously, and stalked out of the door banging it hard behind her. As soon as the door closed, she regretted what she had done. She was such an idiot! And it wasn't as if she didn't know better. She had behaved badly on her very first audition soon after she'd arrived at the Swan and she had vowed never to behave like that again. And now she'd done just that, at what was one of the most important moments in her life. She'd blown it completely by losing her temper.

It was over for her now. Aeysha was going to get the part. She just knew it. She put her hot head against the cool wall. She wanted to feel pleased for Aeysha, but she couldn't. All she felt was jealousy.

Katie watched Georgia leave the building from

across the street. Then she waited for a black cab to pass, crossed the road and walked quickly over to the entrance, where she pushed the buzzer marked Kylight Productions.

"It's Kate Carmichael," she said into the intercom, looking nervously over her shoulder. She felt a bit sick. She was really worried that she would be spotted or, worse still, that she would run into Georgia or Aeysha and then her secret would be out. Both of them had separately asked if she wanted to join them all at lunch over the last couple of days but she had made an excuse on each occasion. She couldn't bear to look either Aeysha or Georgia in the eye.

She walked slowly up the stairs. She knew what she was doing was wrong. She had told herself that she wasn't going to come this afternoon. After she'd been persuaded back to the Swan after the audition fiasco and her mum got the job on *Cinderella* it had been her intention to give up the Zelda auditions. Things were definitely looking up for them both and her mum was transformed. She had given the landlord a piece of her mind and he had immediately sent someone round to do the repairs to the flat. Lily was cooking again and had taken over all the laundry too. Best of all she woke up with a smile and couldn't wait to get to the Swan to work on the designs for *Cinderella*. It felt to Katie as if she and her mum did have some kind of future.

So she had no excuse for carrying on trying to get the role of Zelda. But the lure of playing the part was so strong: it was like being locked in a room with a bar of chocolate when you're starving hungry. It was so hard to resist. . .

Three times Katie had tried to do the right thing, and three times she'd failed. The morning after her mum had announced her good news, she'd knocked on Miss Swan's door to confess, but the headmistress had been too busy to see her and Katie had fled. Then when she was walking down the corridor that morning she had noticed Kylie, in a gaggle of the other girls, staring. It wasn't the first time she had seen Kylie looking at her. She knew that Kylie had been told off by Miss Swan, so what if she was plotting her revenge? If Katie got thrown out of the Swan again, they'd be straight back where they'd started.

Even then she had been determined to do the right thing. But when she had rung Kylight Productions, Poppet had started prattling away before Katie could tell her that she was withdrawing from the auditions.

"How are you, Kate? I know everyone is very excited about seeing you again this afternoon. I know I shouldn't say this, but between you and me I know you are one of the favourites to play Zelda. They all love you."

"Do they?" said Katie doubtfully.

"Definitely," said Poppet. Then she added conspiratorially, "I *really* shouldn't say this but you're my favourite. I think you'd be a brilliant Zelda. You were born for it."

Katie's heart had started racing. How she would love to play Zelda! Maybe she shouldn't chuck it in now when she was so close to the prize. Maybe she should keep her options open for just a little bit longer.

"Anyway, sweetie, what can I do for you?" asked Poppet.

"Oh, nothing," said Katie. "I was just checking that you really were expecting me."

"But of course we are," said Poppet, surprised. "Looking forward to it. You're going to be a star."

A star! It was what she'd always wanted, since she was tiny.

Katie walked up the stairs to the office where she knew everyone was waiting for her. She didn't feel like a star. She felt shabby for the way she was deceiving everyone, but she felt she had to hedge her bets. And there was one thing she really wanted to know: after everything that had happened, was Katie Wilkes-Cox still good enough to get a major role?

Alicia craned her neck and looked back through the rear window of the taxi. She could have sworn that she'd just glimpsed Katie Wilkes-Cox standing in a doorway opposite the Kylight offices. But Katie should be at the Swan. It must have been a trick of the light, thought Alicia, that made one blonde teenage girl look much like another, and because Katie was playing on her mind. Only yesterday morning Katie had knocked on her door and said she'd like to see her, but she'd had to send her away because Sheridan had been on the line demanding to know exactly how big Amber and Theo's names would be on the posters, and she hadn't had had time since then to seek Katie out. Alicia looked at the piece of paper in her hand on which Sheridan had written all the things that it was essential for Theo and Amber to have in their dressing rooms: four bottles of fizzy water, two bottles of still, a bowl of fruit (no bananas), mixed nuts, two cartons of cranberry juice, dark chocolate. Alicia snorted. Theo and Amber would be lucky to have a dressing room at all, such were the cramped conditions backstage at the Swan theatre, let alone free snacks. She sighed. She seemed to be spending more time attending to the demands of her old Swans than looking after the needs of the current ones.

Chapter Twenty

Olivia and Tom were struggling to get into their pantomime horse costume. Will Todd was trying to help, but he wasn't much use because he only had one free arm. A box was tucked under his other.

"What have you got in there?" asked Olivia crossly as Will tried unsuccessfully to ram her leg into the costume.

Will looked around to check nobody was near. "My mice." He opened the top of the box so that Olivia and Tom could see. "They're cute, aren't they?"

"You'd better not let Miss Swan catch you with them," said Tom. "She'll go nuclear."

"I had to bring them in. I promised Connor he could have four and he's going to choose which ones he wants after rehearsal. They keep having babies and my mum says we're going to be overrun by rodents."

"Look out, Will," said Olivia. "Gran's heading this way."

Will looked wildly around. He had to get rid of the box before Miss Swan saw it and asked what was in it. The props table was just nearby so he stuffed the box underneath and pushed it behind the pumpkin that would become Cinderella's carriage during the transformation scene.

He stood up to find Alicia standing right behind him. "What are you up to, William Todd? You look as if butter wouldn't melt in your mouth and that always makes me suspicious."

"Nothing," said Will. "I'm just tidying the props."

"How wonderfully and uncharacteristically helpful of you, Will," said Alicia with a dry smile, and although she looked unconvinced, she didn't ask Will any more awkward questions.

"Ouch," said Tom as Olivia half fell against him as she tried yet again to put her other leg in the horse. Brilliant though the costume was, it was delicate, and getting in and out of it was tricky. It required complete cooperation between the two halves, and Olivia and Tom were not in the mood for cooperating.

"They haven't said anything but I know Ella and Arthur are really hurt that you're not going round to Campion's any more," snapped Olivia. "They know something's up and I'm running out of excuses."

"I never *asked* you to make any excuses for me," said Tom hotly. "Look, Liv, you know I think Campion's is creepy. All the secrecy, the way they keep it like a shrine and the way it makes you behave. Finding out about the children who died was the final straw. I don't want to go there any more and I don't think you should either."

"Ella's just an old lady," said Olivia scornfully. "What harm can she do?"

"Have you asked her about Helen Campion and the two children? They must be related."

Olivia shook her head. "It's not easy. You know how private she is. It feels like prying. But I *am* going to ask her, I promise, Tom. And when I have, will you come back again?"

Tom sighed. "I guess so. But I really don't like spooky stuff."

"But it's Hallowe'en soon! I was going to ask you to help me take Eel and her friends trick-or-treating. Or will you be hiding under the bed instead?"

Tom laughed. "Now, Hallowe'en ghosts are my kind of ghosts," he said. "I'd love to come with you." He smiled at Olivia. "Here, Liv, let me help you put your leg in."

Olivia grinned. She and Tom never fell out for long.

"Is everything ready, Lily?" called Jon from the front of the auditorium. Katie's mum appeared, beaming, her hair and shoulders covered in specks of plaster so it looked as if she had been caught in a snowstorm.

"All ready to go, Jon. I just hope the extra weight of the backcloth on the ceiling isn't too much. The plaster isn't great. But I think it will hold. The worst that can happen is that everyone will get covered in lots of white dust."

"I'll get someone in to look at the ceiling and the roof tomorrow. I've been meaning to get them checked out for ages," said Alicia. "But the backdrops look really lovely, don't they, Jon?"

"Yes," said Jon. "Lily's a real star. Wait till you see her pop-up puppet mice for the transformation scene. They're so cute and clever.

"Poppy!" Jon yelled. She put her head round the side of the wings. "Are all the props in place?" Poppy gave a thumbs-up. He turned to the waiting cast. "OK, everyone. We're going to really try and get Act One up on its legs. Things will go wrong, but don't worry. Let's just try to carry on and get through to the end. Places, please. When you're ready." He sat down and leaned back towards Alicia, who was sitting in the row behind.

"This is going to be very rough, so bear with us, Alicia."

"I will, of course. There's still plenty of time for rehearsals, and I'll make more time in the school day if necessary."

"It's not the Swans I'm worried about," said Jon. "They're always completely professional and some of them are fab. Katie's a revelation, although she seems to be keeping herself to herself a bit. Kylie's a real trooper, and the tinies like Eel and Emmy are terrific, every single one of them. Of course, Livy and Tom will bring the house down. No, it's the principals who are giving me nightmares. Amber Lavelle still doesn't know her lines, and the few she does know she delivers as if they are written very faintly on toilet paper and are being held up for her to see by someone standing at least three miles away."

"Ah," said Alicia, snorting with guilty laughter. "I did warn you. She never was an actor, even when she was at the Swan. We really do try to ensure that all our children can sing, dance and act. It makes them so much more employable. It's what some stage schools call being a triple threat, and it makes sense. But there are some children who really only have one talent. Amber was only ever a singer. Still, if you've got a voice like that, all burned toast and honey, you can get away with a lot. But doesn't Theo's acting ability make up for what she lacks?"

"Yes, Theo's great – when he's here. His prince is devastatingly handsome and utterly charming, and he could do the role walking backwards in his sleep. The real problem," he looked around to check that they definitely weren't overheard, "is that he and Amber have the onstage chemistry of a couple of partially defrosted prawns. Theo is going to have to do an awful lot of acting to persuade the audience that he and Cinders are meant for each other."

"I've every confidence that on the night, and on every night of the run, Theo will convince us all that he and Amber are madly in love; he's nothing if not a pro," said Alicia as the orchestra began to play the overture. There was a small commotion as Sheridan swept into the theatre and settled herself down in an aisle seat with a great deal of look-at-me-I'm-a-very-important-person pomp. Jon sighed. He could do without her being here. It was only a first run-through. He knew that however it went, Sheridan would complain about the way her clients were being treated.

Alicia sat back in her seat and watched. Jon was right, the show was a very long way from ready. But you could see what it might eventually be. Michael Marvell's script was charming but also witty, even when Amber was doing her best to kill it dead. But she sang beautifully, the dancing was lovely and Theo was very charismatic, even though he was clearly treating the whole thing as if it was a gentle stroll

Chapter Twenty-One

Olivia and Tom were in their pantomime horse costume and waiting in the wings for the transformation scene. In the script, the fairy godmother's spell goes awry and Daisy the panto horse steps into the breach and takes Cinderella to the ball. They were all ready to make their entrance. They could see Poppy and the stage management team already trying to move the gilt and glass coach into place, but they had got it wedged tightly against the back wall and were trying to pull it clear with very little space to manoeuvre in. They were whispering furiously to each other but as there was nothing Olivia and Tom could do to help in their costume, they turned their attention to the stage.

The first act was nearing its end. Amber's Cinderella was sobbing by the fire after her sisters and stepmother had gone to the ball. She broke into a beautiful yearning ballad about how much she longed for her mother. It was very affecting. Then there was a puff of smoke and Abbie's Cockney fairy godmother appeared on stage, wand in hand.

"Who are you?" asked Amber with the air of somebody idly enquiring about the time of the next train to Brighton.

"I am your fairy godmother," said Abbie, taking control of the scene, "and you *shall* go to the ball."

"But I don't want to go to the ball. I want my mum," wailed Amber.

"Look, love," said Abbie's fairy godmother. "I can't bring your mum back for you. But I *can* send you to the ball. And what I do know is that your mum would have wanted you to live a little. Not to just sit here snivelling by the fire like a daft pumpkin and feeling sorry for yourself. She'd have wanted to see her daughter making the most of her life."

"Do you think so? Do you really think that's what she would have wanted?" asked

Cinderella.

"With all my heart," said the fairy godmother.

"But I can't go to the ball! I don't have anything to wear. I don't have a carriage and horses."

"Oh, I can help you there, darlin'," said the fairy godmother. "I got a C+ in transformations at fairy school. Have you got a pumpkin?"

"In the pantry," said Cinderella. "I'll just get it."

Amber ran into the wings, where a harassed Poppy, still fighting with the coach, handed her a pumpkin. Amber brought it back and put it down at Abbie's feet.

"Brilliant. Now six white mice. In a box, preferably, or they'll get everywhere. Little blighters."

Amber ran to the wings. "Mice," she hissed at Poppy. "I need the box of mice!"

"Can't you see I'm a bit busy with this wretched coach!" snapped Poppy. "The box is on the floor under the table. Just pick it up yourself."

Amber pouted. The orchestra was getting ready to strike up with the transformation music. Will Todd was holding the cymbals apart and looking for his cue. Irritably, Amber bent down under the table. There were two boxes there. She grabbed the nearest one, ran back on to the stage and placed it at Abbie's feet.

Abbie raised her wand. "Now, Cinderella, remember whatever happens you must be back by midnight, when all your finery will turn to rags. Close your eyes and count back from twelve and your transformation will be complete."

The orchestra began to play, the lights flickered and the stage began to fill with dry ice.

"10 . . . 9 . . . 8 . . . 7 . . ." Abbie touched the pumpkin with her wand, which was the cue for the coach to appear. Nothing happened. Abbie glanced anxiously into the wings. She could see Poppy's distressed face. The coach was completely stuck. She saw Poppy and the others all run round behind it. There was nothing for it but to carry on with the spell.

"5 . . . 4 . . . 3 . . ." Abbie bent over the box and waved her wand. She put her hands on either side of the lid ready to lift it so the six puppet mice could pop out. Tom and Olivia stood ready to gallop on stage. He looked at the box, gasped and opened his mouth to yell,

"Stop!" but at that moment Amber finished her countdown, Will hit the cymbals as loud as he could, the tiered ballgown made from emerald silk dropped from the ceiling over Amber's head and billowed around her like a great sail, and Poppy and the stage managers gave one last huge heave to the coach, which shot like a cork out of a bottle on to the stage and knocked the box over.

There was a tiny shimmering silence and then dozens of little white mice ran all over the stage, squeaking excitedly. One shot straight up Amber's leg, which made her scream loudly. Tom and Olivia galloped on to the stage to try and help, and at that moment there was a terrible crack as if the building itself was breaking in two and a great scar ran like a river across the ceiling of the stage and out into the auditorium. For a moment, everyone watched fascinated, and then the roof fell in.

Chapter Twenty-Two

"Well, it certainly gave new meaning to the saying 'bringing the house down'," said Olivia.

"Amber's screams alone could have done that," said Georgia with a grin. Eel started running around waving her arms about in a wicked impersonation of Amber.

"Stop it," said Tom. "I can't laugh any more. It hurts too much."

"Sheridan was almost as funny the way she stood up on her seat and wouldn't come down. She'd still be there if Theo hadn't carried her out of the building," said Georgia.

"Bet she's sorry she forgot her Gucci handbag," giggled Eel.

"Why?" asked Tom.

"Because when she did eventually get it

back, a mouse had nested inside it." The Swans were hit by another wave of laughter.

"At least nobody was hurt except poor Mr Shaw."

"Fortunately, it's only a minor fracture," said Georgia. "But it means he's out of the panto because it won't be healed in time."

"It'll be Amber's pride that will take the longest to recover. She must have known how ridiculous she looked." Eel did another impression and everyone started laughing again.

Olivia suddenly looked serious. "Actually, though," she said, "there could be problems now. Apparently Sheridan screamed down the phone at Gran, threatening to sue the Swan for every penny it's got. Amber's voice is shot from all the screaming and needs at least a month's rest."

"More likely it's shot from all that talking on her mobile phone," said Eel unsympathetically. "But Amber wouldn't really sue the Swan, would she? It would be like suing your own family."

"She wouldn't have agreed to be in the panto if she didn't still feel something for the place," said Tom.

"I know," said Aeysha, "but I think that something happens to people like Amber when they become stars. They get surrounded by people – agents, advisers, press reps – who bow to their every whim and yet are also quite controlling and then they start to lose touch with reality. Look at Theo."

"Theo's really nice," piped up Eel. "He's paying for us all to go skating. He showed me the tickets."

"He is," agreed Aeysha. "But he still does what Sheridan says, rather than what he really wants. It's obvious he'd much prefer to be playing Baron Hard-Up or one of the ugly sisters, but he isn't because Sheridan said it would be bad for his image."

"But he's a real star," said Georgia. "Stars can do whatever they want."

"I'm not so sure," said Aeysha. "From what I've seen of Amber, Theo, and Cosima and Cosmo last term, it seems to me that the bigger the star you are, the more you're constrained by it. Theo may be the hottest thing at the moment, but how long will it last? Maybe he'll have a long and distinguished career and still be making movies when he's eighty. Or maybe he's reached his peak and the only way is down. It must make you feel really insecure, which might be why stars surround themselves with people like Sheridan who constantly massage their egos but also tell them what to do."

"It's enough to make you want to give up the tap dancing and become an accountant," said Tom gloomily.

"With your maths skills, I'd stick with the tap dancing," said Georgia.

"Well, I'm still going to be a star," said Eel confidently. "And I won't need anyone to massage my ego."

"No," laughed Olivia, "because you can do that very well for yourself."

"I'm sure the whole thing will blow over with Amber, and she'll be back rehearsing next week," said Georgia.

"The show will go on," said Olivia. "It wouldn't be like Gran to let something like this stop her."

But up in the flat that evening, Olivia began to wonder whether she'd been right. She'd gone into the living room to say goodnight and found

Alicia staring pensively into the distance as if in a trance.

"Are you all right, Gran?" asked Olivia.

"Yes, Livy, I'm fine," said Alicia. "I'm just worrying about the panto."

"Why? What's happened?" asked Olivia.

"Well, for a start, Amber has pulled out."

"Is she going to sue you?" asked Olivia anxiously.

"Oh, I think that's only Sheridan's bluster. I reckon Amber would be horrified by the idea."

"So why can't the panto go ahead?"

Alicia gave a long, low sigh. "Because the ceiling is going to take a long time to repair. It's quite a complicated job and we need a specialist builder and I can't find one who can start for two weeks. And that means the dates of the panto will have to be put back and that means Theo can't do it because he's got other commitments and without Amber and Theo as the draw I'm not sure the panto is viable. I can't afford to lose money on it, and the whole point was to make a nice big contribution to charity."

"But can't we find an alternative venue?"

"Even if we could at this late stage, it would cost too much," said Alicia. "I've been racking my brains but I can't come up with a solution. Still, maybe if I sleep on it something will come to me."

"I wish . . . I wish we had a fairy godmother who could make it all come right," said Olivia.

Alicia hugged her granddaughter. "I don't believe in making wishes. I believe in making things happen."

Olivia said goodnight to her grandmother and padded off to bed. She lay awake for a long time, thinking about Alicia's sad face and brave words. Making things happen! She wondered if she could.

Chapter Twenty-Three

Alicia beamed at Georgia and Aeysha.

"It's good Zelda news," she said. "For both of you."

As she said the word "both", a strange expression crossed Georgia's face as if she was disappointed rather than pleased. Aeysha nudged her and grinned and put her arm around her, hardly noticing Georgia's stiff shoulders and pasted-on smile. Alicia was so delighted she didn't notice anything amiss either.

"I can't believe it," said Aeysha, shaking her head as if she was trying to wake herself up.

"Me neither," said Georgia quietly.

"Well, it's true," said Alicia. "I don't know what you did at the last audition, Georgia, but Poppet mentioned that it was your display of spirit that clinched it for you. Well done."

Georgia's stomach churned. She thought she had blown it and instead she was through to the next stage!

"Well, girls, you're the last two Swans standing. I'm very proud of you. Well done and keep at it. Maybe one of you will be lucky. You both deserve it, and whatever happens you must remember that you've beaten off hundreds, maybe thousands, of other girls to get this far. Even if neither of you do get it, it should give you both such a confidence boost for the future."

"When will the next audition be?" asked Aeysha.

"It'll be a screen test this time, and they'll let you know directly. Oh, and they had these couriered over for both of you." Alicia gave a thick cream envelope to each girl. "Read it all thoroughly but make sure you keep checking your phones too. You don't want to lose the role through carelessness," said Alicia. "I've seen that kind of thing happen. A missed audition or a missed rehearsal and suddenly that big chance slips away. Now, off you go, girls, and good luck to you both."

As soon as they got outside Alicia's office,

the girls tore open their envelopes. Inside were cards congratulating them on getting so far and a single sheet of paper with a speech from the script that they were told to learn by heart. The two girls went to the cloakroom to get their things. Katie was there, just finishing a phone call, and when she saw Georgia and Aeysha she looked embarrassed and scuttled away.

"What's got into her?" said Georgia, looking after Katie with a puzzled expression on her face. Katie seemed more isolated than she had been at the beginning of term, not less. But Aeysha was on the phone to her mum sharing the good news. Georgia left her mum a message. Aeysha finished her call and put her phone down on one of the benches so she could fling her arms round Georgia.

"It doesn't feel real, does it?" she said.

Georgia shook her head. "I wonder how many girls are left in the running. I wish we knew. Then we'd know what we were really up against."

Aeysha suddenly hit her own head. "I'm such a numpty! I've left my music for tomorrow in one of the practice rooms. Will you wait for me? I won't be a tick and then we can catch the bus together." She danced off.

Georgia sat down heavily on the bench. She needed a moment alone to deal with her conflicting emotions. She knew that she should be thrilled for herself and for Aeysha, who was her friend, one of her best friends, in fact. Before this moment she would have confidently said that she would do anything for Aeysha, from giving her all the red sweets in the fruit gum packet even though she liked them best, to pulling her from a burning building even if it put her in peril herself. Aeysha had always been a good and loyal friend to her. But now they weren't just friends, they were rivals – and rivals for the same plum part. If Miss Swan had said that she had got through to the next round of auditions but Aeysha hadn't, she would have been completely devastated on her friend's behalf and full of genuine sympathy. But somehow it was harder to feel pleasure for Aeysha's success when potentially that success might mean her own failure. Only one of them could get the role. It was so confusing. Her phone rang, and she answered it.

"Georgie darling, it's Poppet from Kylight Productions. I've suppose you've heard the good news. We need you to come and see us again tomorrow for a screen test. Ten a.m. Is that OK?"

"Yes, that's good," said Georgia. "Miss Swan told Aeysha and me that we were still up for the role. We're both made up."

"Lovely," said Poppet. "Actually, is Aeysha there? The director wants to see her at two thirty p.m. tomorrow."

"She'll be back in a minute," said Georgia. "I could give her a message."

"Could you, darling?" asked Poppet. "That would be too, too sweet of you. Tell you what, you tell your friend, and I'll just send her a text with confirmation. No need for her to get back to me, unless there's a problem."

"OK," said Georgia. "Poppet, do you know how many girls are still up for Zelda or is that a trade secret?"

"I probably shouldn't tell you, darling," said Poppet, "but I don't see the harm in it. You're down to the last three. You two from the Swan and a girl called Kate Carmichael. Oops, there I go again, giving away state secrets! Forget that name immediately. Must dash, sweetie. See you tomorrow, and don't forget to tell Aeysha.

I'll text her now."

Georgia put the phone down. Just three of them. So close and yet so far. She had a sudden revelation: if she wasn't going to get it, she would actually prefer the unknown Kate Carmichael to get the role instead of Aeysha. Then at least the two of them could commiserate together. But if Aeysha got it and she didn't, she'd feel so jealous she didn't think she could bear it.

Aeysha's phone gave a little bleep announcing the arrival of a text. Georgia reached for it and then snatched her hand away as if the phone might scald her. The she picked it up with trembling fingers. She could see that the message was from Poppet. She swallowed hard and it was as if a great struggle was taking place inside her. Then she pressed the delete button and immediately felt terrible, hollow and empty, as if she had somehow lost an essential part of herself. She placed the phone back on the bench just as Aeysha walked into the changing room and began to gather up her things.

"I wonder when we'll hear about the next audition," said Aeysha.

"Oh, I don't know. Maybe not for days yet," replied Georgia, and she flushed red as she said it and her heart gave an unexpected lurch.

"Come on," said Aeysha, "or we'll miss the bus."

Chapter Twenty-Four

The bus turned the corner and came to a stop.

"I'll get off with you here, Georgie, and walk the rest of the way. It's not far," said Aeysha. "And it'll give us a bit more time together."

As they got off the bus, she linked arms with Georgia. Georgia suddenly burst into tears. The girls stopped walking and Aeysha stared at her.

"What's wrong, Georgie? You should be on top of the world. We're both through to the next round. You could be Zelda! Why are you crying?"

"Because I hate myself," sobbed Georgia.

"Why?" asked Aeysha in a puzzled voice.

"I can't say. It's too horrible," wept Georgia. "I've done something really terrible.

You'll never forgive me."

"Of course I'll forgive you, you're my friend. Friends always forgive each other."

"Not when they've done something this bad."

"Georgie," said Aeysha patiently. "Unless you've suddenly turned into a serial killer and have body parts stashed in your sports bag, I can't imagine what you could have done that's so terrible."

Georgia closed her eyes for a second. "I haven't given you the message that Poppet gave me about your recall audition tomorrow at two thirty p.m.," said Georgia in a voice so tiny that Aeysha had to strain to hear her.

There was an electric pause and then Aeysha took a deep breath and said, "But you have now, Georgie. You've done the right thing. So it doesn't matter."

"But I did something even worse. Poppet texted you too, and I deleted it because I wanted you to miss the audition."

"Ah," said Aeysha quietly. "That is quite bad. That's old-Katie-Wilkes-Cox bad." There was a long silence and then she added, "But I haven't missed it. You've 'fessed up. So it doesn't matter, Georgie."

She went to hug her but Georgia pulled away. "But it matters to me. It matters to me that I'm turning into such a horrible person, a person who even feels jealous of her best friends. I can see you're not jealous of me; you seem as genuinely pleased about my success in the auditions as you are for yourself. But I'm jealous of you, Aeysha. And it's not just you. When Livy announced that she wasn't going to go up for Zelda, I felt so relieved. I wasn't sorry at all. I was thrilled. I was so worried that she would, and that she would get it rather than me because if anyone was born to play Zelda, it's probably Livy. I was pleased she wasn't auditioning; it felt like one less rival to contend with, one less person I was going to have to beat if I was in with a chance of being Zelda."

"But you don't think that about all the other girls who have been auditioning from other schools for Zelda, do you?" said Aeysha slowly, as if she was thinking very hard. Georgia shook her head. "It only becomes a problem when your friend is also your rival, doesn't it?"

"Yes," said Georgia. "I don't mind about all the other girls. I don't know them." She started sobbing again. "But if I'm honest, what I feel is even worse still, Aeysha. If I can't get the part, I'd almost prefer one of those other girls to get it than you. I'd feel better now there are just three of us in the running if the girl we don't know got it and we both failed together, than if you got it and I was the one who lost out." Her eyes were blazing and her face was pale. "There! I've said it. I've said what I really feel, and now you know just how despicable and what a horrible human being I am." She sank on to a low wall nearby. Aeysha sat down next to her and took her hand.

"But, Georgie, what you feel is natural. Everyone feels jealous of other people. Remember how Livy felt in Edinburgh during the summer when Evie suddenly appeared on the scene? With us, it's even worse because I'm one of your best friends. That's the problem with this business – our friends aren't just our friends, they're also our rivals. It's tough."

"But most people don't act on their jealousy," said Georgia. "They might feel those things but they don't try to spoil their best friend's chance like I did."

"Oh, I don't know," said Aeysha. "Maybe

if they had the chance and maybe if they thought they could get away with it and never be found out, maybe they would. Maybe we all would. Me included. Maybe you're just being honest in admitting it. My mum once told me about some writer who said, 'Whenever a friend succeeds, a little something in me dies.'"

"Ugh, that's horrible," said Georgia with a shiver. "But it's even more horrible to think it might be true."

"Look at it this way. You'd be pleased for me if I got selected for the England netball team or I got a book published, wouldn't you?"

Georgia nodded vigorously. "Of course I would."

"Exactly," said Aeysha. "Because you don't want to write a book or be really good at netball. The Zelda thing is only a problem because we're both trying to win at the same thing. Oh, this whole audition business is such a horrid process. The more I do it the less convinced I am that it's really for me."

"But you still want to play Zelda?"

"Yes," said Aeysha. "But if I don't, and you do, I will be genuinely pleased for you. Really."

"I feel better," said Georgia. "It was killing me not being able to say how I felt. I felt like a bottle of fizzy drink that had been shaken hard but not opened." She smiled at Aeysha. "And if you get it and I don't, I really will try to be pleased for you too. But it may be a bit of a struggle for me."

"That just shows what a nice person you are, Georgie."

They walked in companionable silence for a minute until they were outside Georgia's house. "Aeysha, do you think you *would* like to write a book one day?"

Aeysha thought for a moment. "I think I would," she said seriously. "But I can tell you one thing I know for certain: I'm never going to get selected for the England netball team."

Chapter Twenty-Five

Olivia, Tom and Eel stood outside the block of flats and peered nervously through the door.

"It's really posh," hissed Eel. "It's even got a doorman. Actually, it's got two. Actually, they look less like doormen than human guard dogs. I bet you didn't think of that."

Olivia made a face. She hadn't thought Theo's apartment block would be quite so grand. She had imagined it would be like any other block of flats, which had the numbers of the flats and sometimes even the names of the residents with an intercom by the front door of the building. She had been worried that when they rang the bell Theo would be out, or that he wouldn't want to talk to them at first, but she had never envisaged that they wouldn't even be able to get near him.

Despite their fancy clothes, the doormen looked as fierce as Rottweilers. Getting past them wouldn't be easy. One was sitting at a desk watching CCTV footage of the corridors of the building and the other was meeting and greeting visitors. The children watched the entrance for a few minutes and saw several people enter. It was clear that they were being asked for their names before the doorman rang ahead to see whether he should let the people up.

"Maybe we should just go in and say that we're expected," said Tom.

"But we're not," said Olivia reasonably. "He won't even talk to Gran. Sheridan rang to say that Theo was withdrawing from *Cinderella*, and he hasn't returned any of Gran's calls since. Which I think is really rude and cowardly."

"But he did send her that enormous bunch of flowers with a message that said how sorry he was," said Eel. "You could tell the flowers were incredibly expensive because they were really exotic colours and looked incredibly evil. One of them is bright red and spiky and looks just like Sheridan when she's in a bad mood."

"Which is always. I bet she chose them,"

said Olivia gloomily. "I bet he doesn't even know he sent them. It's all just for show. It doesn't mean anything." Then she added furiously, "I thought Theo was better than that."

"Look," said Tom, convinced that Olivia was about to begin on another tirade about Theo's lack of loyalty to the Swan and her gran, who had done so much to help his career. "Why don't I go in, give my name and see if I get in? If I do, then we can get you two in too."

"I don't know," brooded Olivia. "We lose the element of surprise. It's so easy to say no to somebody when you don't have to do it face to face. I just thought that if we could see him, we'd be able to persuade him to change his mind." She looked thoughtful. "I wonder if there's a back entrance to the building."

"It'll be locked," said Tom.

"Worth a look," said Olivia. They walked down a small side street to the back of the building. The sky was overcast and there was a bite to the wind as if it was warning that winter was on its way. They found the back door, which was, as Tom had guessed, closed and locked from the inside. They looked up at the building as it rose above them. High above ground level some of the flats had balconies with window boxes and gaily coloured flowers.

"They haven't got a very nice view," said Olivia. "You're just looking on to the side of the department store next door."

"Look, that one's Theo's," said Eel, pointing excitedly upwards to a balcony on the third floor.

"How can you possibly know?" asked Tom curiously.

Eel smiled confidently. "Look what he's using to grow his flowers in."

"Tap shoes," said Olivia excitedly. "I think you're right, Eel. And look, that flag waving outside is the Elsinore flag. Remember we saw it, Tom, when Gran took us to see Theo play *Hamlet* at the National Theatre. It *must* be Theo's flat." She looked around and her eye fell on an open window in the department store opposite. It was on the same level as Theo's balcony and through it they could just glimpse a woman looking into a mirror as she put on her lipstick. Olivia's eyes lit up. She glanced at the window to the ladies' loo for a bit longer and then back at the balcony as if assessing something.

Tom suddenly looked worried. "I know

what you're thinking, Liv Marvell, and you'd better think again," he said.

"But it's definitely possible. I can hook the wire over the rail of the balcony and, providing I can find somewhere to attach the wire in the Ladies', I reckon I could get across easily enough," said Olivia.

"Too dangerous, Liv. It's different when it's a matter of life and death, but this isn't. Why don't we just lay siege to the building and ambush Theo when he goes in or comes out?"

"Because he'll just leap into a taxi and brush us off," said Olivia.

"Tom's right, Livy. It's much too dangerous to walk the high-wire to the balcony," said Eel, and Olivia could see the anxiety in her little sister's eyes.

"We have to think of something else," she said frowning.

"Hey, what are you three doing here?" said a familiar voice.

Olivia, Eel and Tom spun round.

"Kasha!" said Tom, and he and Kasha grinned and gave each other a high-five. No one had seen Kasha since Edinburgh, and that was before his chart success. Eel squealed and gave him a hug. Kasha looked over to Olivia and smiled. He had always had time for Olivia Marvell.

"Hi, Livy," he said softly. "How you doing?"

Olivia suddenly felt shy. Last term Kasha had been at school with them, but now he seemed incredibly grown up. During the summer when he had been with them at the Edinburgh Fringe Festival, he had just been Kasha. Now he had a number-one single and was famous. Girls screamed at him. He suddenly felt a world away from them. He looked different too. He was wearing shades even though it wasn't at all sunny, he had his coat collar pulled up and a woolly hat pulled down.

"I'm fine," she said. "But are you planning to rob a bank or something?"

Kasha grinned and removed his dark glasses. "Looks like it, doesn't it? I keep expecting to get arrested." He sighed. "But it's the only way I can go out at the moment. Since the single went to number one, I'm jumped on everywhere I go. You know, I used to dream about being famous, but I never thought about not being able to walk down the street or pop out to get a coffee without people wanting a piece of you. I even went out with a false beard and walking stick the other day. I can tell you I was thanking Sebastian Shaw for all those acting lessons; they've come in super-useful."

"But surely you've got what you always wanted? Are you complaining about your glamorous life, mate?" asked Tom good-naturedly.

"No," said Kasha. "I know I'm dead lucky and I'm loving every minute. But I would like to be able to pop out to buy a bag of crisps or go out with a girl without somebody taking a photograph."

"We all saw the picture of you and Abbie in the paper," said Tom.

"Is Abbie your new girlfriend?" asked Eel.

"Eel!" said Olivia, embarrassed by her sister's directness.

"No," said Kasha. "Abbie and I have known each other forever. We started at the Swan on the same day when we were seven. We were both so nervous we hid together in the cupboard in the girls' cloakroom and Miss Swan had to coax us out with chocolate."

"And now you're a pop star and Abbie will probably be famous too when her movie is out next year," said Eel.

"But I just still feel like me," said Kasha seriously, and Olivia thought that he suddenly looked very young and vulnerable. He was only a couple of years older than her. "Anyway, you lot haven't answered my question. What are you doing here? You look as if you're staking out this block of flats."

"We are, we're staking out Theo Deacon," said Eel, and she quickly explained about the Swan panto, the roof falling in and Theo's withdrawal. "Livy thinks we might be able to persuade him to reconsider."

"If we could only get to talk to him face to face," said Olivia.

"Liv," said Tom, "is stupidly keen to walk the high-wire across to his balcony from that window. Eel and I were just trying to stop her."

Kasha shook his head. "For a bright girl you sure have some daft ideas, Livy. I'd hate you to die so young. It would be such a waste."

"I wasn't planning on falling, and anyway do you have a better idea?" asked Olivia hotly.

Kasha grinned. "Actually, I think I do. Is

Pablo still teaching *castells* at the Swan?" They nodded. "Good. Time to mobilise. It's Saturday tomorrow. Do you think you can get everyone to come down here?"

They nodded again and Olivia said delightedly, "Kasha Kasparian, you're not just a pretty face, you've got brains too!"

"I know," said Kasha with a grin. "But, Livy, even if you can persuade Theo to do the panto, you still don't have a theatre."

"I know," said Olivia looking serious. "But Gran and I are working on that. Maybe the sensible thing would have been to say it's impossible and just give up. But I wanted to make something happen, and I can only do that one piece at a time. It's like building a *castell*; each individual piece or person has to be exactly in the right place to build something taller and stronger."

Chapter Twenty-Six

The next day, Will and Connor were having a great time staking out the entrance to Theo's block. They had both dressed for the part and were wearing dark glasses and raincoats. Will had even borrowed his dad's trilby hat but Olivia had confiscated it, pointing out that they were supposed to be blending in with the crowd, not drawing attention to themselves. A taxi drew up at the entrance, and Theo and Sheridan got out and hurried into the building.

Will called Olivia on his phone. "White Mouse to Olivia. Suspect has just entered the building."

Olivia ignored the White Mouse nonsense and heaved a sigh of relief. They had been hanging around in the cold all morning. They'd arrived early, only to see Theo leave his flat almost immediately. Some of the Swans were getting a bit restive but fortunately they were all delighted to see Kasha again, who, much to the Swans' delight, had come armed with signed CDs of his single for all of them. It was, thought Olivia, odd how somebody who the Swans had all been used to seeing every day during the last school year had now taken on such an aura that several of the younger girls were reduced to giggling and blushes when Kasha spoke to them. She had been worried that Theo might not come back for the rest of the day and all their waiting would have been in vain, and that they might not get another chance to speak to him after today.

"Is he alone?" she asked Will down the phone.

"No, Sheridan's with him," said Will. Olivia sighed. Sheridan would be an added challenge.

"OK, Will, keep watching and if you and Connor see either of them leave, let me know ASAP." She put her phone in her pocket and turned to the assembled Swans.

"Right, it's now or never."

* * *

Up in the flat Theo and Sheridan were arguing.

"The Swan made me what I am today. Without it I'd be nothing and be nowhere. I feel such a rat for letting Alicia and all those kids down. I'll never be able to look any of them in the eye again," said Theo.

"Well, you won't have to," said Sheridan. "I'm dealing with them. Look, Theo, the script I promised you has been couriered over. It's in my bag. They want you very badly and are prepared to pay. It's perfect. A fabulous cameo. Three weeks' filming and then the other project you were waiting on can slot right in afterwards after the Christmas break. Just put the Swan right out of your head."

"I'll never do that," said Theo. "There is something called loyalty, Sheridan."

"I'm loyal to you, Theo, and to my other clients. I do what I think is in your best interests. You're at the top of your game and it's my job to keep you there. It's a tough business, you know. For every one of you, there are ten thousand or a hundred thousand would-be Theo Deacons out there, waiting tables and dreaming. You get no brownie points for being nice. Now, I've no time for sentimentality. Let the Swan go, Theo. You owe it nothing."

Theo said nothing. He felt so torn. He knew he owed Sheridan. She had turned his career around when it had seemed to be going nowhere. But he also felt that he owed the Swan.

Sheridan saw his face. "Here, read this," she said, throwing the script to him. "It's very classy. It'll put a smile back on your face. They need a decision quickly, so read fast, although I already have, so you can just skim the first few pages."

Theo picked up the script and opened it. He read the first few pages. Sheridan was right. It was a plum part, but he couldn't concentrate. He kept thinking he could hear the sound of children laughing outside in the street, something that always reminded him of the Swan.

"I'll go into the other room to read it," he said.

In the street below, Pablo was marshalling the Swans.

"Everybody ready?"

"Yes," they chorused.

"Good, because once we begin, we'll be blocking the road, my little ducklings, and that won't make us popular. You're so experienced now, you should be able to make this *castell* in one single seamless movement; it should be an easy one for you, only six tiers." He eyed the balcony before turning to Olivia and Eel. "Once the structure is in place, you two will be able to climb to the top and swing on to the balcony with no problem. Right, everyone. Places." The children who formed the base of the *castell*, known as a *pinya*, moved into their places. "Next tier," called Pablo, and children climbed on to the shoulders of others.

The structure began to rise into the air like a wedding cake. The third tier of children climbed like mountain goats up on to the shoulders of the other Swans. When the fourth tier began to take their place the children at the bottom of the pyramid, who had all been selected for their strength and dependability, shifted slightly with the pressure. A ripple ran through the entire structure. Pablo looked a little anxious. It was a critical moment, but the *castell* settled again. Pablo signalled for the next tier of children to climb, and the structure flowed upwards as if like magic. A couple of people who were walking down the street stopped to watch and take pictures and they clapped as the final tier of children took their places. Pablo then nodded at Olivia and Eel, who both climbed to the peak of the *castell* with such fleet-footed certainty that they seemed more like mountain goats than children.

In the flat, Theo was engrossed in reading the script. He had to admit that Sheridan was right. The part was a gem, small but crucial to the plotting and beautifully written. The sort of cameo that might just get you a best-supporting-actor nomination at the Oscars. He noted that Sheridan had cannily pencilled the figure being offered on the front of the script, no doubt as an incentive. It was breathtaking. He carried on reading.

Sheridan smiled to herself. She was certain that Theo would take the bait. She'd get a very juicy fifteen per cent of his fee too. She might even buy herself another Gucci handbag. She suddenly became aware that something was happening outside in the street and, checking to see that Theo was undisturbed, she made her way to the balcony's glass doors. She pulled back the muslin curtain, slid open a door and stepped out on to the balcony just as Olivia and Eel emerged over the top.

Sheridan scowled at them and did a double-take as she looked over the edge and saw the *castell* melt away. Several of the Swans waved at her, and Kylie Morris and some of her friends shouted, "Hey, Sheridan!" and when the agent glared at them they produced mouse ears. Sheridan turned puce with rage and Olivia tried not to laugh. She had to say one thing for Kylie: she had a wicked sense of humour. Olivia and Eel moved towards the door. Sheridan stepped in front of it.

"Not so fast, young ladies," she hissed. "Theo's not in. And if he was here, he wouldn't want to see you. It would do no good anyway. You're wasting your time. He signed up for the new movie an hour ago."

Olivia felt crushed. They were too late. She turned to signal to the Swans to make another *castell* so they could get down. But Eel didn't move.

"How do we know you're not lying?" asked Eel loudly. "You said he's out, and we know he's in. We've got the front staked out. You were seen entering together, and no one's seen Theo leave. Our man on the ground would have texted us if he had. You say he's signed a movie deal but I won't believe it until Theo tells us that himself, and that he doesn't want to do the Swan panto."

"Are you calling me a liar, little girl?" said Sheridan nastily. "Go away, both of you, and stop bothering Theo or I'll call the police. You do realise that you're trespassing? It wouldn't look good for your beloved stage school to have that splashed all over the paper."

"Are you blackmailing us?" asked Eel, a steely edge to her voice.

"Call it what you want," said Sheridan, "but I won't be held to ransom by a load of stage-school brats."

"Two can play at that game," said Eel. She flipped open her phone. "It looks so much better in HD, of course."

It was a video of Sheridan standing on one of the seats in the Swan theatre. Her mouth was wide open and she was screaming, her normally perfect hair covered in dust, so she looked like the deranged survivor of some comical cosmic catastrophe. "It's perfect YouTube stuff. It might even go viral."

"You little rat," shouted Sheridan, making a grab for the phone. Olivia looked at her little sister. She had no idea that Eel had taken the video. Eel was behaving as badly as Sheridan; her only excuse was that Sheridan was at least thirty years older than her and should know better. Olivia made a decision. If the only way they were going to get Theo back into the Swan panto was by behaving like this, then it wasn't worth it. She was certain that her gran would be horrified if she knew that Eel had met blackmail with blackmail.

"I'm sorry," said Olivia. "We made a mistake. We shouldn't have come. . ." She tailed off. Her throat felt raw. "My sister will delete the video, I promise. If you say Theo is out, he's out. I apologise for us both." She leaned over the balcony and nodded to Pablo. "We'll leave the way we came in," she said quietly.

"Which I assume was by parachute," said Theo, who had appeared soundlessly on the terrace behind them. He walked to the edge and peered over as the *castell* began to rise in the air. "Hey, that's even more amazing than a parachute."

The Swans whooped and laughed and broke into a spontaneous rendition of "Please Please Me", putting their hands together in a beseeching gesture and going down on their knees.

Theo grinned broadly. He looked at Olivia and Eel. "I guess you've come to give me a ticking off. You'd better come in."

"You can't just invite in anyone who tries to bludgeon their way into your home, Theo," hissed Sheridan.

"No," agreed Theo reasonably. "I can't. But Olivia and Eel Marvell aren't just anyone. They're my friends."

Chapter Twenty-Seven

Theo sat alone in his flat, thinking. He had sat there so long that night had fallen and the street lamps had come on. He shivered. There was a real chill in the air. It felt as if snow was on the way.

Olivia and Eel had been persuasive, even more persuasive after he had sent a protesting Sheridan away and said that he would call her later.

"We really don't have a chance of making it happen without you, Theo," said Olivia softly. "You'd be keeping the chance alive. If you say yes, it may help us find a theatre."

"Yes," said Eel. "We'd all love you forever, Theo, and go and see all your movies, even if we thought they sounded really boring like that last one you did, which had all that silly kissing stuff in it."

"Eel!" said Olivia. "You're not helping."

"Actually," said Theo with a grin, "Eel's right. I'm fed up of romcoms. I want to do something meaty."

"There you are," said Eel. "You should do *Cinderella,* and now Amber's out of it and poor Sebastian too, you could play who you like, even Cinders, but I wouldn't advise that cos she's really soppy. At least, Amber made her seem soppy. You could be Baron Hard-Up! If you played Baron Hard-Up, Jon would let you do as much tap dancing as you wanted."

Theo smiled. "What would Sheridan say?"

"But it's your life, Theo, not Sheridan's," said Olivia seriously.

"Yes, but she's supposed to be looking out for me." He sighed. "I don't know. I'm very tempted by your offer." And he was. Like the movie cameo, Baron Hard-Up was a small but beautifully written role with lots of comedy. "But where would we perform?"

"Gran's still trying to find somewhere," said Olivia. "She's put out lots of feelers, and

I've got an idea of somewhere that might work but I have to tread very carefully."

"So," said Theo slowly, "you're asking me to turn down the movie and loads of dosh and commit to something that might never happen, that's just a pipe dream?"

"In a nutshell, yes," said Eel. Then she added, "But dreams do sometimes come true."

Olivia had looked at him very seriously with her compelling dark eyes and said simply, "It's an act of faith, Theo. It's about making something happen."

"All right," said Theo. "I'm not promising I'll do it, but I am promising to think about it."

"Thank you," said Olivia. She and Eel got up to go.

Theo stood up too, and handed Eel an envelope. "You'd better take the tickets for the skating . . . just in case I don't see you again before. . ."

But although Eel's eyes lit up when she saw the envelope, she shook her head firmly. "No, Theo. You keep them. Think of it as an act of faith. That I believe you're going to be there in the panto and be there skating with us at Somerset House."

* * *

After they had gone, Theo did what he had promised to do and thought hard. Olivia and Eel were right. The Swan panto would collapse as surely as the theatre roof without his presence. It made Theo feel needed. One of the things he knew about his profession was that however famous you were, you were always replaceable. If he didn't sign up for the movie, somebody else would. It wouldn't just be cancelled. But if he dropped out of *Cinderella*, that would be the end of it. Sheridan might say that the movie people wanted him really badly and the amount they were prepared to pay for a cameo reflected that. But he also knew that if he said no, they'd just move on to the next actor on their wish list.

But what if this movie was his big break? The business was full of stories of actors and actresses who had turned down plum roles that had then been the making of someone else. And what if he said no to the movie, and then *Cinderella* couldn't find a theatre? He'd have turned down a perfectly good opportunity for nothing. He sat in the fading light, his mind drifting, and he remembered being back at the

Swan and sitting in Alicia's office. He'd been sixteen going on seventeen and he'd just been turned down for a place at every leading drama school in the country. He had always been a bit of a golden boy at the Swan and he had thought he was going to stroll into RADA, but he hadn't even got past the first audition. He was devastated and completely demoralised.

He had railed for a while and Alicia had listened quietly and said little, until he said, "That's it. I'm giving up, there's no point in going on."

There was a pause.

"Yes, maybe you should, Theo," said Alicia quietly. "If that's what you want."

Theo had stared, astonished, at Alicia. It was as if she had just thrown a hand grenade into the room. He had expected Alicia to protest at his intention to give up on acting and tell him how talented he was.

"But . . . but . . . but . . ."

"Look, Theo," said Alicia, "if you're going to let the first knock-back affect you so badly, then maybe acting isn't the profession for you. It's hard out there. Maybe you'll be one of the lucky ones; maybe you won't. But you won't know unless you try it and make things happen for yourself. If you don't believe in yourself, nobody else will. You've got to get out there and work, Theo, because nobody is just going to hand everything to you on a plate. Go out there and do it, or don't. Apply to RADA again next year, or don't. But don't whine about it. It's your choice. You always have a choice."

"You always have a choice," murmured Theo to himself. Well, he was making his. He rang Sheridan and spoke to her swiftly and firmly for a couple of moments. He went and made himself a cup of tea and as he carried it towards his chair, his phone rang. Sheridan's name flashed up on the screen. He was tempted not to answer, but he was glad he did.

"How unexpectedly obliging of them to offer more time," he said.

As soon as the call finished he called Alicia. "You have very persuasive granddaughters. Count me in on *Cinderella* but on three conditions," he said. "I want to play Baron Hard-Up and I want a tap solo with a *42nd Street*-style chorus behind me, and you need to find a venue by midnight on Hallowe'en. That's the cut-off point. Otherwise I'll do the movie."

Chapter Twenty-Eight

Georgia ran up the steps of the Swan, whistling. It was very early, only just gone seven thirty a.m., but she had arranged to meet Aeysha to rehearse their dance for the panto and it was the only time that a studio would be free. She had a good feeling about today. It had been two days since the screen test, and it felt as if she had been keeping all her fingers and toes crossed ever since. She knew her mum had too, even though Lydia kept warning her not to get her hopes up too high. But she was certain she would hear something today.

"Please," she thought, "please let it be me." She so wanted to play Zelda. She had done right from the moment Miss Swan first mentioned the auditions. But of course she hadn't really had the confidence to think that she really would. It seemed like an unreachable dream, as remote and unlikely as her mum winning the lottery, or being picked to be the first child in space or discovering that in fact she was a child wizard with special magical powers. But as time had passed and she had kept being called back she had began to dare to dream that she might actually get it. She felt like a long-distance runner with the winning line in sight, and to fall at this point would be too, too cruel. She didn't even want to think about it. She hurried towards the girls' cloakroom, and as she did she saw somebody peer down the stairs and call her name. It was Miss Swan. Her face was unreadable.

"Georgia dear, will you step into my office a moment."

Georgia took a deep breath. This felt like her date with destiny. She walked swiftly up the stairs and into Miss Swan's cosy office. Her fingers and toes were tingling.

Alicia didn't mince her words. "There's no way to break this gently. I'm afraid it's bad news about Zelda, Georgia. You haven't got it. I'm sorry. I know it's very disappointing and you're going to be very upset, but you did extremely well to get so far."

Georgia felt numb. She had never felt about a role the way she felt about Zelda. She wanted to scream her frustration out loud. She tried to hold back the tears so that she would look professional, but a big fat one rolled down her cheek, leaving a salty trail.

"Aeysha?" she whispered.

"Still in the running," said Alicia. "It's just her and another girl left."

"Kate Carmichael," said Georgia. "I bet she's a blonde," she added fiercely.

Alicia looked momentarily surprised at the name, and then the expression of someone who has just discovered the missing piece of a jigsaw under the sofa flitted across her face. "Carmichael? You're sure she's called Kate Carmichael?"

"Yes," said Georgia. "Do you know her?"

"I sincerely hope not," murmured Alicia.

"I'm pleased for Aeysha. I hope she gets it," said Georgia. "I really do."

"That's very generous of you, Georgia, particularly in the circumstances. But I never expected anything less of you. You would have been a lovely Zelda, but there will be other opportunities for you, and I'm going to offer you one now."

"A job?" asked Georgia, and she suddenly perked up.

"Yes," said Alicia, "but I'm afraid it's not a paid one, or as high profile as Zelda. And it's not completely certain yet. But I think you'll be pleased."

"What is it?" asked Georgia.

"Jon would like you to play Cinderella in the Swan panto. Amber's not coming back and now Theo has agreed to be a tap-dancing Baron Hard-Up if we can find a theatre, we need to find a new Cinders from the school."

"Me? You want me to play Cinderella!" said Georgia breathlessly, her eyes shining.

"Yes, Georgia. We're offering you the role. We had already decided even before I heard that you hadn't got Zelda. It's a really big opportunity for you. Provided of course we do go ahead. The Swan has never had a show that didn't go on. We're doing everything we can to make this happen."

"Oh," said Georgia, pink-cheeked. She suddenly thought of something.

"So who will play the prince?"

"Kasha Kasparian has kindly agreed to take the role. It will be quite a Swan reunion."

"Me? Playing Cinders opposite Kasha?" Georgia blushed pink and her eyes shone. "Oh, thank you, Miss Swan. This is almost better than Zelda."

"Just remember it's not certain yet. Unless we find a theatre in the next few days, nobody will be going to the ball." Alicia's mobile rang. She glanced at it, and smiled at Georgia. "That will be Theo. Again. He's desperate to hear that we've found a theatre."

Georgia grinned. "Not as desperate as me, Miss Swan."

Chapter Twenty-Nine

Olivia and Tom jumped off the high-wire on the Campion's stage. Ella and Arthur clapped.

"Tea?" asked Ella.

"Yes, please," replied Olivia and Tom. They put the flickering ghost-light back in its place centre stage and followed the two old people through to the kitchen at the back of the building.

"It's nice to see you again, Tom," said Ella. "I thought we had frightened you away."

Tom blushed and looked a little uncomfortable.

"So how are rehearsals for the pantomime going?" asked Arthur. "Ella and I are looking forward to seeing you do your pantomime horse routine."

"Ah," said Tom. "I'm not sure you are going to be able to." His eyes were signalling frantically at Olivia. It was now or never. They couldn't expect to get a better opening.

"The thing is," said Olivia, "we've had a setback. The roof of the Swan theatre fell in. It's going to take ages to repair and we don't have another venue. So unless we can find somewhere else to perform *Cinderella* we won't be able to do it. It's a pity after all the hard work that's gone into it."

There was a tiny silence.

"That's a shame," said Ella evenly.

"Of course, if we could just find somewhere else," said Tom. "But it's hard. . ."

"We wondered," said Olivia, "if it might be possible to use Campion's? It would be so perfect. The theatre is just sitting here, it seems such a shame not to use it, and we'd be so careful with everything."

Ella looked at Olivia as if she had gone mad. "You mean put on public performances again at Campion's Palace of Varieties?" The old woman's eyes blazed. "Impossible! Over my dead body. How dare you! How dare you wheedle your way in here, trying to take over my theatre, stirring up the ghosts?"

"But we didn't," said Tom helplessly. "We found Campion's by accident and you invited us in."

"Because when I saw you walking the high-wire, you reminded me of somebody," said Ella.

"Of Lizzie and Davey?" asked Olivia very quietly.

Ella stared at her, white-faced and with blazing eyes. "What do you know about them?" She drew herself up and her eyes flashed dangerously. "You know nothing. Nothing at all. You've been poking around like spies, trying to find out my business. You've got your eyes on Campion's, haven't you? You're trying to get it from me like he did. You're spies for him, aren't you?"

"No," said Olivia helplessly. "We don't want to take Campion's from you. We just want to use it for a few performances of *Cinderella*. For charity. Nothing more."

"It's just a trick," said Ella. "You're trying to trick me out of Campion's."

"I'm sorry," stuttered Olivia. "We should never have asked. I didn't realise how much it would upset you, Ella."

"Get out! Get out and never come back," cried Ella, and she fell back against her chair, clutching her heart.

"Ella!" Olivia and Tom leapt to their feet, scared.

"She'll be fine," said Arthur quietly. "She has these funny turns when she gets agitated. But it's best if you two go."

Olivia and Tom hurried out into Hangman's Alley. The street was gilded with frost and glittered in the darkness.

"What was all that about?" asked Tom. "Did she just go completely mad?"

"I don't know," said Olivia, shaking her head.

"Do you think she was having a heart attack?"

"No," said Olivia. "I think that Ella's heart is already broken. I just wish we could mend it for her."

Chapter Thirty

Katie was passing reception when she heard Mrs Gibbs call her name. The school secretary had a letter in her hand.

"This came for you," she said, holding out a cream manila envelope with foreign stamps all over it. "It looks as if it's from South Africa. Do you know anyone in South Africa?"

Katie's heart began to thud. Her mouth was dry. There was only one person that it could possibly be from. Her father. Part of her desperately wanted to know what the letter said and part of her wanted it to spontaneously combust in Mrs Gibbs' hand so she would never have to read it.

"I expect it's from my cousins," she said with a bright smile. She'd always been good at lying but it still surprised her how easy she found it. She reached for the letter, half expecting it to burn her hand.

She stuffed the letter in her bag and made her way up to the little studio at the top of the school, which she knew would be empty. She put down her bag and looked at herself in the mirrored wall. The face that stared back at her was a pretty one with serious, anxious eyes. She laid her head against the glass and whispered, "Who are you? Katie Wilkes-Cox? Kate Carmichael? Katie Nobody? Katie Somebody? Katie Liar?"

Her phone rang. She let it go to voicemail. When her phone bleeped to tell her that a message had been left, she pressed a button to access it. She recognised the voice immediately. It was the director of the *Zelda* movie. She could hear the barely suppressed excitement in his voice.

"Kate, it's Doug here. Call me back as soon as you can. I need to talk to you. I've exciting news for you."

Katie stared at the phone in her hand as if it was about to explode. Doug's message could only mean one thing. She had got it. She had got Zelda! She should be screaming with happiness but she just felt empty, wrung out. All the skulking about to get the role, all the lies, all the pretence, made her feel tired rather than triumphant. It was as if jumping all the hurdles and overcoming all the obstacles had become the purpose rather than reaching the finishing line in a winning position. She didn't feel like a winner. She felt as if she was a loser. She had barely had time to get used to the new Katie Wilkes-Cox and already she had mislaid her.

She reached inside her bag and pulled out the letter. What could he want with her? Why would he get in touch after everything that had happened? She held the letter a little away from her as if it was an unexploded bomb as she ran her thumbnail under the flap of the envelope and pulled out a sheet of paper. She recognised the writing immediately. She took a deep breath and began to read the letter.

Dear Kitten,

I bet you'll be surprised to hear from me after everything that's happened. To be honest, I'm quite surprised to be writing this. It wasn't hard to find out that you were back at the Swan. After everything you did for them, I guessed that's where you'd go. I hope they realise that my little girl is doing them a big favour. I wish I could understand your attachment to the place. It's a little two-bit stage school; it can't contain you, not somebody of your looks and talent. You're better than the Swan. Which is why I'm writing. I miss you, Kitten. I miss your spark, the way you make things happen. You and me, we're two peas in a pod. Together we could be a great team. There are opportunities here in South Africa. It's a go-getting place and you and me, we could go-get together. So here's the deal. You come join me and we'll embark on Project Kitten: turning Katie Wilkes-Cox into a global brand, a massive star. Don't think you'll have to live in poverty. I managed to get away with a couple of million. Had it squirrelled away in a Swiss bank account against hard times. Not a lot, I know, but together we can turn it into a billion. Think about it. The world's your oyster. Get in touch, Katie. Ring the number below and I'll get right back to you.

Dad

Katie stared at the letter. She couldn't believe

what he was saying. Her father lived in his own delusional bubble. Anger began to rise in her throat. He had money. Two million pounds! And he talked about it as if it was loose change, while she and her mum had been living for months in a way that made every extra two pounds seem like a lottery win. To think she had once admired him, and had aspired to be just like him: someone who lied and cheated to get wherever he wanted to be. She shuddered. She felt as if she had just had a very lucky escape.

Katie stood up, walked to the window and opened it wide, and then she hauled herself up on to the sill and crouched there, the skyline of London spread out in front of her. She tore the letter into tiny pieces and threw it into the wind, where it whirled like confetti and made Katie think of snow. When she had shredded the final piece, she jumped back off the sill. As she did so, her phone rang. It was Doug again. She pressed answer. The news he was giving her felt all the sweeter because she had already made her decision, made her choice.

After she had finished her brief call with Doug, she curled up on the floor like a baby.

After a few minutes, the door of the

rehearsal room swung slowly open. Miss Swan was standing there, leaning heavily on her stick. Katie sat up and looked at her questioningly.

"Mrs Gibbs seemed to think you might be heading in this direction. She told me she had given you a letter. From South Africa. From your father, I imagine," said Alicia.

Katie nodded.

"I feared as much. Do you want to come down to my office and talk about it?"

Katie nodded and stood up.

"The letter?" asked Alicia, when they were settled in Alicia's office.

"He wanted me to join him in South Africa," said Katie fiercely. "He said he could make me a star."

"And are you going to?"

Katie shook her head vigorously. "I tore it up into a million pieces."

"Probably the best thing for it," said Alicia softly. "Although I expect the police might have wanted to take a look. He *is* a wanted man."

"There was a mobile number. I memorised it," said Katie.

Alicia smiled. "Clever girl." She paused for a moment and then she said, "I've been wanting to have a chat with you in any case. I thought you might be able to shed some light on the mysterious Kate Carmichael."

Katie's eyes darkened in fear. "It's not what you think, Miss Swan. . ." she said urgently, but then tailed off. She gave a massive sigh. "Maybe it is . . . but it's not quite . . . I can explain."

Alicia smiled a forgiving smile. "I don't doubt for a minute that you can, Katie." There was a slight pause. "I think that when you first returned to the Swan I underestimated how difficult things were for you. Since your mother has been working on *Cinderella*, she's confided in me a bit and I've an inkling of how hard life was in those early weeks both at home and here at the Swan. I think I may have failed you, Katie, and pushed you towards taking some ill-considered decisions. Looking back, I think there may have been a couple of times when you tried to confess and I wasn't patient enough with you, or ready to listen because I was too taken up with unimportant things. I'm sorry."

"I'm the one who should be sorry," whispered Katie. "I've let everyone down. You, the Swan, my mum, myself."

"We all make bad choices, Katie."

"Yes," said Katie, tears sliding down her face. "But I keep making them. I think I must just be a bad person."

Alicia took her hand. "You know that's not true, my dear. When I asked you to leave the Swan almost a year ago it was as much because of your dad as it was because of you, and because of the example he set you. Your reaction to the letter proves that you've turned your back on walking all over people just to become a star. But there's something more. I had to ask you to leave the Swan last year because it was clear to me that you weren't really sorry for what you did to Olivia and Georgia; you were only sorry that you'd been found out. Something has changed in you, Katie, and it's a change immeasurably for the better."

"So you're not going to ask me to leave the school?" whispered Katie.

"Not if, as I suspect, you are really sorry and you've made the right choice about Zelda. I assume I'm correct in thinking that you've got the role?"

"Yes," said Katie. "I did get it. But I'm not going to do it. I've told them. I want to stay here and learn everything I can and have proper friends and work so hard that I will become a great actress when I'm older. I want people to say that Katie Wilkes-Cox is a name to be proud of, not ashamed."

"Well," said Alicia, "in that case you'd better tell me about how you came to make your wrong decisions so that I can make some right ones."

Chapter Thirty-One

Olivia, Tom and Eel were walking towards the Swan. It was almost nine o clock at night and bitterly cold. They had just walked Emmy Lovedale back to her house after a marathon trick-or-treating session. Olivia and Tom had been supervising a very excited Eel and three of her friends as they collected enough sweets and chocolate to give them toothache for days. Afterwards they had all gone back to the Swan, where Alicia had fed them sausages and mash with eyeball jelly for pudding. The green jelly with lychees suspended in it looked a bit too realistic for Olivia.

It had only started snowing when they had left the Swan to walk Emmy home, but already London had been transformed into a winter wonderland. The flakes were huge, great white moths fluttering around the street lamps, and it had quickly settled like a white blanket over the streets, muffling the sound and making London seem eerily peaceful. Everyone seemed to have retreated indoors and the three children felt as if they had London entirely to themselves.

"It's beautiful," said Eel as she held out her hands to catch the flakes.

"It is," agreed Olivia, "but it's far too early for snow."

"If the snow has come early, maybe Christmas will too," said Eel. "I've already written my Christmas list. I don't think I can wait until the twenty-fifth of December."

"What have you asked for, Eel?" asked Tom.

"Chocolate. Tickets to see the Royal Ballet do *Swan Lake* at the Royal Opera House and more chocolate."

She took a huge bite from one of the many bars she was carrying.

"You'll be sick, Eel Marvell, if you eat any more chocolate," said her sister.

"But I've got tons of it!" she said. "I love Hallowe'en. I love trick-or-treating." She skipped happily ahead and started scraping together snow from a parked car to make a snowball.

"I'm glad somebody's happy," said Olivia moodily.

"Liv," said Tom, "you've done everything you possibly could to try to save the Swan panto. So has your gran. Maybe it just wasn't meant to be."

Olivia kicked at a little mound of snow that had banked against a lamppost.

"I just thought I could make it happen. I really thought that when Ella realised how important it was that she'd let us use Campion's. Instead I've just made her angry and upset."

"You've not heard anything from her or Arthur?"

Olivia shook her head. "No, I slid our note saying sorry under the back door, and left the flowers we bought. But there's been nothing. I feel awful. Gran always says that it's worth asking for what you want because even if the person you ask says no, you're in no worse a position than you were before. But in this case we are. We've upset Ella and we still haven't got a theatre for the Swan pantomime and in two or so hours' time it will be too late because Theo will sign up for his movie."

"I heard your gran say that he's already rung three times today asking if there's any news."

"It just shows how much he wants to do *Cinderella*," said Olivia. "He's itching to get into rehearsals."

"Maybe he'll hold out against Sheridan another few days."

"I don't think so," said Olivia gloomily. "He gave us the chance to make *Cinderella* happen and we failed." Her voice cracked with emotion. Tom hugged her.

"And there's something else," she whispered. "The dreams have stopped."

Tom raised his eyebrows. "But that's a good thing, isn't it?" he said.

Olivia frowned. "I don't know. It's as if some kind of connection has been broken." Her eyes filled with tears. "It makes me think we're never going to see Ella and Arthur and Campion's again."

Tom went to give her another hug but at that moment a snowball whizzed past her right ear and hit Tom full on.

"Right," said Tom with a grin. "You're going to regret that, Eel Marvell!" He gathered up some snow and chased after her. He thought Liv probably needed a moment or two alone.

Olivia watched the two of them throw snow around. She looked down a side street and saw a gaggle of witches and skeletons, led by a taller grim reaper, walking away in the distance. It was a strange sight in the empty city. The silence was eerie, as if the whole of London was holding its breath, broken only by Eel's indignant screeches as Tom stuffed a snowball down her neck. Olivia shivered and stamped her feet. Tom threw a snowball at her but she didn't respond so he continued pelting Eel, who eventually collapsed into the snow, gasping with laughter and begging for mercy. When she finally stood up, she was shivering uncontrollably.

"I'm freezing," she said.

"Me too," said Tom, rubbing his hands together. "Let's get moving."

"We can cut down Henley Street under the bridge and past the end of Hangman's Alley," said Eel. "It's much quicker."

Olivia and Tom glanced at each other.

"Bit spooky down there at this time of

night," said Tom evenly.

"Please. . ." said Eel. "I'm so cold I think I've caught pneumonia." Her teeth were chattering.

Olivia nodded brusquely. "If you're sure."

"Come on then," said Tom, and they began walking as briskly as they could through the thickening snow. They passed the Tube station, cut through another side street and headed down Henley Street. They had just got to the railway bridge when Olivia suddenly stopped and stood very still. Her face was puzzled.

"Did you hear that?" she said.

Tom and Eel looked at her blankly. "I didn't hear anything," said Eel. "Come on, let's get home."

"There it is again," said Olivia. Tom and Eel looked at her. She was perched on one foot with her head to one side like a bird. "Children laughing."

"It's the wind, Livy," said Eel. The snow was falling faster and thicker. It was turning into a blizzard, dancing in front of their eyes.

Olivia shrugged and said doubtfully, "Maybe you're right."

They ran, sliding on the ice under the railway bridge, but as soon as they reached the other side, Olivia skidded to an abrupt halt.

"There it is again! It's definitely children. I can hear them, and . . ." She stared at Tom and Eel, white-faced, "they're not laughing any more, they're crying."

Tom looked worried. "It's just trick-or-treaters somewhere in the distance," he said.

"Then why can't you hear them?" asked Olivia seriously.

"I want to go home," said Eel. "You look strange, Livy. Like a ghost. Are you teasing us, Livy, because if you are, I don't like it."

"Come on, Liv, we're almost home. Down past Hangman's Alley and then it's no distance at all." Tom tried to pull Olivia along but she wouldn't budge. She was standing as still as a statue and listening intently. Suddenly a look of panic came over her face and she broke into a run. She called back over her shoulder to the others. "We've got to go to Campion's. There's something dreadfully wrong, I know there is!"

"Liv! Liv!" called Tom. "Come back!" But she didn't stop. He turned to Eel. "We'd better go after her."

They ran as fast as they could in the snow, following Olivia's footprints until they turned sharply up Hangman's Alley. Olivia was standing by Campion's faded entrance, banging her fists against the door and calling, "Ella! Arthur!" Her voice echoed across the white, empty street.

"Liv," said Tom, touching her shoulder.

She jumped and shook him off. "Get off me, Tom! There's something wrong. I know there is!"

"What about the back door?"

"The door to the passageway is locked. We can't get in that way." Olivia banged again on the door.

"What's going on?" asked Eel in a small voice. "You're scaring me, Livy."

Tom put his arm round her. A black cat suddenly yowled and appeared from nowhere behind them, making them all jump.

"It's no good, they can't hear us," said Olivia despairingly. She stepped back from the door and looked up at the little window. It was shut. "I'm going to climb up and see if I can force it open."

"Liv," said Tom urgently. "You might not

get a warm welcome from Ella if you just turn up uninvited. She's already told you to stay away."

"It's a risk I'm just going to have to take," said Olivia, and she began to scramble up the drainpipe. "Wait for me here. If I'm not back in five minutes, call the police." She quickly reached the window sill, brushed the snow away and heaved herself carefully on to it. She stood up against the window and found a gap at the top just big enough to get her fingers in. She leaned down on it and as she did so, one of her feet lost its grip, the other slipped as if in solidarity and for a heart-stopping moment she was hanging from the window by her fingertips.

Eel screamed and the sound reverberated eerily around the alleyway. Olivia found her footing and pushed the window again. Perhaps because it had already taken her weight, it shifted easily. She pushed it down and climbed inside. She moved soundlessly past the old bar area. The whispering in her head was urging her on. She could see the glimmer of eggshell blue and gilt, but she could smell something too, something that shouldn't be there: a strong smell of burning. Campion's was on fire!

Chapter Thirty-Two

Olivia ran frantically on to the horseshoe balcony. The fire was small and she could see immediately how it had started. The ghost-light had been placed too close to one of the stage curtains and now the curtain was smouldering gently, waiting to burst into flames and send the whole theatre up in smoke. The flames would lick up the ancient walls and across the roof and the diamond chandelier would come crashing down in the blink of an eye.

Olivia raced down to the stage, screaming, "Ella! Arthur! Fire! Fire!" She tugged at the curtain to try and pull it down, hoping it would fall and smother the flames that had suddenly spluttered into life and were quickly licking upwards. But the curtain didn't budge. Olivia cursed Arthur's sturdy handiwork as she felt the heat of the flames on her face.

She looked around wildly and her eye fell on the high-wire. She leapt on it, took a deep breath and then ran at top speed towards the curtain, trying to gather all the momentum she could. As she reached the end of the wire she made a flying leap upwards. For a moment it seemed as if she had misjudged her jump and would fly into a wall of flame, but she landed on the curtain just above the flames, although rather too close for comfort.

Olivia began to haul herself up the curtain, just ahead of the curling flame, aiming to make it to the top and wrench it from its fastenings before she was consumed by the fire. She felt the warmth tickling ominously at her feet and smoke was beginning to billow all around her. Its acrid taste hit the back of her throat and made her choke. It was getting harder and harder to breathe.

Olivia glanced down at the advancing flames. She heaved herself up with one last stupendous effort and reached desperately for the curtain fastening. She was no longer just trying to save Campion's, she was trying to save her own life too. There was a sudden roar of ravenous flame as the fire really took hold, a loud cry and the curtain tore away from its fastenings and fell down to the stage with Olivia still clinging to it. She opened her mouth to scream but was shocked into silence by the icy water being poured over her head.

"More tea?" asked Ella.

"Yes, please," said Alicia. They were sitting on the horseshoe balcony overlooking the stage. The smell of singed material was still very strong, but with the exception of the curtain, there was no other fire damage. Alicia gazed around her at the gilt and eggshell-blue interior, the massive mirrors and the chandelier with its hundreds of crystal drops.

"It's so exquisite," she said. "You know, I think it's the most beautiful theatre I've ever seen, and I've seen a few in my time. It's amazing to think that this gem has been hidden away all these years. It's extraordinary, and you've kept it so beautifully. It must have been a real labour of love."

"Yes," said Ella quietly. "It has been." She looked at Olivia. "And if it hadn't been for Livy, it would have all gone up in smoke, and Arthur and me with it. I have a lot to thank you for, Livy. You were very brave. It was all my fault too. I came in here, moved the ghost-light so I could sweep the stage and then remembered I'd put a pan of milk on to heat. I went back into the kitchen and then to bed and quite forgot about leaving the ghost-light so close to the curtain. I'm getting old and forgetful."

"Well, thank goodness that nobody was hurt," said Alicia. "Although when I got Tom's call telling me there'd been an accident in Hangman's Alley, my heart was in my mouth. Are you sure you don't want me to call a doctor, Livy?"

Olivia shook her head firmly.

"She's as tough as old boots," said Tom. "We'll have to call her Nine Lives Liv."

"It was just lucky that Arthur poured that bucket of water over me when he did." Olivia grinned. "Things were getting a bit hot. At least what was left of the curtain was thick enough to break my fall."

"What I don't understand," said Eel, "is how Livy knew that something was wrong in the first place."

Olivia said nothing; she just glanced quickly at Ella.

"Just good luck, I suppose," said Alicia. "Although, from what Olivia says, Campion's was playing on her mind. Maybe it was her unconscious that drew her here. Perhaps what some people might call sixth sense?"

"Perhaps," said Eel curiously. "But she kept saying she could hear children's voices telling her to come here when we were down by the railway bridge in Henley Street. Tom and I couldn't hear anything but she was very insistent. It was as if she was getting a message. But the really strange thing, when you think about it, is that at that point the fire couldn't even have broken out."

"Ooh, spooky," said Tom, trying to make light of it. "But it is Hallowe'en, after all."

"Yes," said Olivia, looking directly at Ella. "It is Hallowe'en. And tonight when I heard the children they weren't laughing, they were crying."

"Oh, it was probably the wind carrying the distant sounds of trick-or-treaters," said Alicia breezily. "I think we can safely say it wasn't ghosts. There's always a scientific explanation for these things."

"By Henley Street railway bridge, you say?" said Ella softly.

"Yes," said Olivia, and she saw that Ella was staring at her very hard. The church clock struck a quarter to midnight.

"Ella, we must go," said Alicia. "How did it get so late? Thank you for the tea and thank you for allowing me to see your beautiful, beautiful theatre."

Ella stood up. "It's I who should thank you. Without Livy, Campion's would have burned to a cinder." She turned to Olivia. "I want to give you a thank-you present. I want you and the Swans to perform your production of *Cinderella* here at Campion's. The whole run, as many performances as you like. It's my gift to you." She looked around the theatre. "It's time to put out the ghost-light and welcome real performers back on to the stage. Campion's is open for business again."

Everyone looked at each other and broke into peals of delighted laughter.

Theo was pacing up and down in his flat.

"It's almost midnight, Theo," said

Sheridan, looking at her phone. "I said I'd ring on the dot and let Hollywood know that you'll do it."

Theo gave an unhappy sigh. "I just really thought that Livy and Alicia would pull it off. They're not the kind of people to be beaten."

"Ah," said Sheridan sagely. "Maybe luck wasn't with them. Never mind. The Swan's loss will be Hollywood's gain. . ." The church clock in the square beyond began to strike midnight.

"Right," said Sheridan with a happy smile. "I'm making that call." She went to press a button on her phone and at that moment Theo's mobile chirped into life. Alicia's number flashed on the screen. He held it to his ear.

"Theo! It's Livy. You will go to the ball, after all! We've found a theatre. The most magical theatre in the entire world!"

Theo gave a yelp of pleasure and his face was suffused with a rosy glow of happiness. Sheridan stood watching him for a moment as he talked excitedly into the phone, and then she picked up her new Gucci handbag and walked out of the flat without even saying goodbye.

Chapter Thirty-Three

Ella pulled out a photograph and showed it to Olivia and Tom. Olivia guessed immediately who it was. The photo was black-and-white and yellowing at the corners. But the three people in the picture – a young woman and two laughing children – looked full of life, as if they might just step out of the photo any moment and say hello. But Olivia knew that they had been dead for more than fifty years.

"My sister-in-law, Helen, and her twins, Elisabeth and David," said Ella. "My brother's children. He was a bomber pilot in the war before he was shot down and killed. After that, Helen and the children came to live with me at Campion's, even though I told them that they'd be safer in the country. But they wouldn't hear of it. They loved Campion's. All three of them. Lizzie and Davey played hide-and-seek and 'it' all over the building. The children had their own special seats right in the front of the balcony. They'd sit there for hours, watching everything that was taking place on the stage. They acted in several Campion's shows over the years. It was in their blood. Helen had been a dancer here before the war. In fact, I couldn't have kept the place open during the war without her help. Those children never stopped laughing, not even when the bombs fell and we had to run to the Tube station and take shelter on the platform. They thought they were invincible."

She pulled out another photo. "Here they are in their sailor suits as the Babes in the Wood. Oh and look, here they are walking the tightrope; not that they were ever as good as you and Tom, Livy. But when I first heard you laughing and glimpsed you on the wire, I thought that they had come back to me. Here they are in *Cinderella* too. I played Cinders and Helen was the fairy godmother and Lizzie and Davey were the white mice and assorted villagers." Her eyes brimmed with tears at all the memories. "I suppose I hoped that one day Campion's would be theirs to look after and cherish just as my brother and I had inherited and looked after it."

"Ella, you don't have to tell us any more," said Olivia.

"No, I want to. I need to," said Ella. She took a deep breath.

"The three of them died six years after the war. An unexploded bomb had been dropped during the war but rolled down the embankment by the Henley Street railway bridge into the undergrowth so nobody realised it was there. It could have gone off at any moment. But it didn't: not until midnight on Hallowe'en nineteen fifty-one, when Helen and Lizzie and Davey were walking past it. They were the only casualties. Killed instantly. And it was my fault."

"But, Ella, it was an accident. You couldn't possibly have been to blame. It was just terrible bad luck that they were there when the bomb exploded."

Ella dabbed at her faded eyes with a tissue. "But they were coming to find me at the Tube station. They were worried about me. I was late back from a night out at the Glass Slipper. I'd promised I'd be home much earlier and when

I didn't come back they got worried and came looking for me. If I'd come home when I'd said I would, they'd probably all three be sitting here today."

"The Glass Slipper? I've heard that name before," said Olivia. "Gran mentioned it. It was a club, wasn't it?"

"Yes," said Ella. "One of those new-style places that sprung up after the war when everyone fell in love with all things American. People were fed up with the past. They wanted brand-new shiny things. Campion's had done fine during the war but afterwards people turned their backs on it. They thought we were an Edwardian relic with our old-fashioned pantomimes and music-hall-style entertainment. They wanted something racier, something more sophisticated. Within a couple of years of the war ending we were in trouble. We were going to go under. I didn't dare tell Helen and the twins. I was desperate. Campion's had been in our family since it first opened; I couldn't bear to think that I might be the one to lose it."

"But you didn't lose it. It's still here, and you've really looked after it and lavished it with love," said Olivia.

"Yes, but I closed it down. You were right, Olivia, when you said that I turned it into a museum or a shrine. I was angry when you said that but you *are* right. A theatre isn't a theatre unless it's used. It's just another building, slowly falling into disrepair as you try to hold back the ravages of time. A theatre needs actors, an audience, dancers, orchestras, otherwise it's taken over by the ghosts. I gave Campion's to the ghosts; I gave it to the dead."

"I still don't understand why," said Olivia.

"Because I fell in love with a man who I thought loved me but who only wanted to take Campion's from me. His name was Hugo Prince. He was handsome, debonair and the owner of the Glass Slipper. He turned up here one night. There was almost no one in the audience. He was smart; he must have realised immediately we were in financial trouble. He showed an interest in me, asked me out for a drink. I was flattered. I'd been married to Campion's for such a long time. I was in my thirties by then and I didn't think I'd ever have a real relationship. But he seemed like the answer to all my dreams, a real-life Prince Charming. Hugo courted me, said he wanted us to get married and that he wanted to invest in Campion's. He assured me that he wanted the place to stay the same. Livy, I can't tell you what a relief it was. I knew how important it was to Helen and the twins that Campion's carried on. And I loved Hugo. Or at least I thought I did. So we got engaged."

"What happened?" asked Tom.

"On the night Helen and Lizzie and Davey died, I went to meet him at the Glass Slipper. I arrived a little early; he was in the supper area talking to the punters. I thought I'd surprise him and so I slipped into his office. I don't know why, but I hid behind a curtain. A few minutes later he came in, but he wasn't alone. He had his business partner with him and they were talking about Campion's and their plans for it, how as soon as we were married he was going to rip the heart out of it and turn it into a chrome and leather banquette supper club like the Glass Slipper and bring in American singers and cocktail waitresses."

"Did you confront him?"

"No," said Ella sadly. "I was too much of a coward. I just left my engagement ring on his desk and walked out. I wandered around the streets for hours in a daze. I felt so betrayed. I don't think he ever loved me at all; it had just been a pretence to get his hands on Campion's. He wanted the name and the premises. I lost track of time. It was only when I heard the clock striking midnight that I realised how much time had passed and that Lily and the children would be worried sick about where I was. I caught the Tube and hurried towards Hangman's Alley. As soon as I saw the ambulances and fire engines at the bridge I knew immediately. Campion's has been closed from that day to this."

"Did Hugo Prince ever try to contact you?"

Ella shook her head. "That's how I knew it wasn't love."

"So you've been alone ever since."

"Just me and Arthur. He was the stage manager and he refused to leave, even though he knew I couldn't pay him. Oh, and of course, the ghosts have been here with me too."

"Ella," said Olivia slowly, "do you think that it's time to let them go?"

Ella nodded. "Perhaps. Perhaps you and Tom were sent to set them free."

"But it was just an accident that Tom's

glider flew in through the open window and we found Campion's," said Olivia, frowning.

Ella smiled dreamily. "Believe what you want, Livy, and give an old lady the comfort of believing what she wants."

Out in the auditorium, some of the Swans and Theo were getting ready to run through a scene from *Cinderella*. The whole atmosphere of Campion's was so magical that Jon was in raptures about its potential. Katie's mum had been overcome with joy when she had discovered the old Campion's backcloths that had been used for their productions of *Cinderella* since the nineteenth century. Most of them were too delicate to use any more, but she had been busy making careful copies and had suggested to Ella that she should contact a friend of hers who worked at the Victoria and Albert Museum and who could help in preserving them.

"They'll be fascinated by all your stage equipment too," she'd told Ella. "It's extraordinary."

Ella had smiled. "Just as long as it stays in the theatre and doesn't end up in a museum. I want Campion's to come back to life. I want it to live again. *I* want to live again."

And the thing was, it *was* coming alive. The Swans were busy all over the building, rehearsing or helping to bring the neglected areas beyond the stage and auditorium back to life. Even Theo was helping sweep and clean, and he had never looked happier. He tap danced as he worked.

Eel and some other Swans were helping Alicia clear up the bar area, which was thick with dust and cobwebs. Eel was standing on a chair rubbing hard at an old mirror and making it sparkle.

"You're doing a good job there, Eel," said Tom encouragingly.

"I know," said Eel. "I am."

"Livy, could you help me?" asked Katie shyly. "I want to move this chest to get behind it. The skirting board is filthy."

"Of course," said Olivia.

Katie had seemed so much more relaxed over the last couple of weeks. She was no longer cutting herself off from the others, and often came and sat quietly with Olivia, Tom, Georgia and Aeysha, not saying much but smiling at their chatter.

The chest was heavy to shift. "Are you looking forward to the skating the day after tomorrow?" asked Olivia.

Katie nodded. "It'll be brilliant. But I'm not great at it. I always need someone to hang on to or I'll fall over."

"We all need someone to hang on to," said Olivia softly. "You're not the only one."

"Livy," said Katie urgently. "I want to say thank you. You and Tom and the others, you've all been—"

Olivia put up a warning hand. "Don't say anything, Katie. You're part of the gang now."

At that moment, Georgia appeared at the door to show everyone her ballgown.

"Oh, Georgie, you look just like a princess," said Eel.

Georgia glowed.

"As pretty as a picture," said Alicia softly. Several Swans broke into a spontaneous rendition of "One Day My Prince will Come". Georgia blushed. She was loving playing Cinderella, except for one thing: it was going to be so embarrassing having to kiss Kasha in front of all her friends. The Swans gathered around Georgia, serenading her and making her blush all the more.

Katie watched her from a little distance. She was genuinely pleased that Georgia was going to play Cinderella. She had sensed how important getting Zelda had been for Georgia, and, as she had told Alicia when the whole sorry story of her involvement in the Zelda auditions had tumbled out, one of the things she felt most guilty about was that she might have deprived Georgia – the only other blonde in the running – of her big chance by her actions.

"I feel as if I've somehow cheated her," said Katie sadly. "And she's always been so nice to me."

"Even if you hadn't been picked, Georgia might not have got Zelda," said Alicia. "We can speculate but we'll never know. Listen, Katie, you could confess, but why upset Georgia? She's happy playing Cinderella. Sometimes things fall out for the best."

The crowd of Swans around Georgia melted away, leaving Katie alone with her.

"You're going to a brilliant Cinderella, Georgia. The best, the very best Cinderella in the whole world," said Katie fiercely. "And you *so* deserve it."

Georgia smiled. She was touched by Katie's good wishes but slightly puzzled by her intensity. It was as if it really, really mattered to her.

Chapter Thirty-Four

"Listen," said Aeysha. "I need to talk to you. I've got something to tell you all." The others looked at her expectantly.

"You didn't! You got it! You're going to play Zelda, aren't you?" squealed Georgia excitedly.

Aeysha shook her head, her dark eyes serious. "No, I didn't get it," she said quietly. Georgia burst into tears.

"Aw shame, Aeysha. I'm really sorry," said Tom. The others nodded their heads sympathetically.

"So that other girl must have got it? Kate Carmichael?" said Georgia.

Aeysha shrugged. "I guess so."

"You should have got it," said Georgia

loyally. "I bet you were the best."

"It doesn't matter if I was the best or not," said Aeysha. "I wasn't right for the part, or at least the directors and the producers didn't think I was right for the part. And that's what counts. They're the ones who have the power and they're the ones who decide."

"Oh, Aeysha, I'm so sorry," said Olivia, giving her friend a hug. "When did you hear?"

"More than a week ago," said Aeysha. "But I didn't tell you all because I knew you'd all be disappointed for me and in any case I wanted to do some thinking and talk to my mum and dad and Miss Swan."

"About what?" asked Georgia.

"Look," said Aeysha. "I don't think there's any easy way to put this. I wanted to talk about leaving the Swan." If she had punched them all in the stomach and then asked them a really hard maths question the others couldn't have looked more shocked.

Georgia burst into tears again. "Leave? You can't leave! The Swan? Us?"

Aeysha hugged her. "I don't want to leave you, Georgia. Or you, Tom, or Livy. You're my friends. The very thought of it makes me want to cry. But I've thought about it, and I know it's what I've got to do."

"I don't understand," said Tom.

"Aeysha," said Georgia tearfully. "You can't let not getting one poxy role make you give up. That would be so stupid. You can't throw away your career like this. You're really talented. Everybody knows that. Even Miss Swan would tell you that, and she never tells people to their face how good they are."

Aeysha held Georgia's hand and smiled. "She has told me. She was very kind about my abilities. But even Miss Swan knows that in this business talent isn't enough. You need other things too: self-belief, an ability to bounce back from rejection, a hunger for it. Most of all what you need is luck."

"What Gran always calls 'a little patch of sunlight'," said Olivia.

"Exactly," said Aeysha. "When she called me in to see her, she said I wasn't to feel rejected because actually it's almost nothing to do with me and almost everything to do with whim – perhaps even what the director had for breakfast on the morning of the final audition or whether he was too hot or too cold. That in this instance the sun hadn't shone on me. But that if I continued to work hard and I was lucky it might on another occasion."

"So, see, it will. I know it will and I bet Miss Swan does too," said Georgia. "You don't have to give up because you didn't have the luck this time. Your number will come up."

"Or maybe it won't," said Aeysha quietly. "Maybe I'll never have my little moment in the sun. Lots of actors don't, do they? We always hear about the ones who do make it, who get the Hollywood movie deal or star in the West End. But what about all those who don't? The ones who mostly don't get chosen. Who endlessly wait in line to be seen at auditions, sometimes come close, but then never get the part. That's what it's like for most people in the biz. They have the talent and the dedication, they just never have the luck. That little patch of sunlight."

"But you have to keep trying," said Georgia plaintively. "You can't just give up."

"Look," said Aeysha. "That may be right for you, Georgia, and it is for an awful lot of people in theatre and show business, but it's not for me. Maybe I don't want it enough, but in any case wanting something doesn't mean that you're going to get it. Wanting isn't enough. Otherwise all those people on those TV talent contests who say that it's their dream would win. But they don't, because they can't all win. What I do know is that I don't want to spend my life waiting to be chosen by somebody else and not having any control over it. I want to be able to make things happen for myself. If there's one thing that this audition process has taught me, it's that I don't like feeling powerless. If you study really hard for an exam, you know you're likely to be rewarded by a good grade. Of course, there's some element of luck in whether the questions you've revised come up. But if you've put in the graft, on the whole you get the result. Auditions aren't like that at all. You can have all the talent in the world and you might have put in the practice but you still might never be the one that gets chosen."

"You really *have* been thinking about this a lot, haven't you, Aeysha?" said Tom.

Aeysha nodded. "Yes, I have, and for some time now. And the more I've been involved in the audition process for Zelda, the more I've realised that it's not for me. I love acting, and singing and dancing. I love being here at the

Swan with you lot. But I also know that I can't live my life waiting to be chosen, filling in with jobs behind bars or in call centres, waiting for my lucky break to come along."

"What are you going to do?" asked Olivia.

"Well, I'm going to stay here until the end of the school year, and I'm going to enjoy every single minute of it. We'll be starting our GCSE courses next year so that's the moment to go somewhere else, to a school where I can do a wider range of subjects than I can here, and where I can spend the time I currently spend on singing and dancing working out what I really want to do with my life. Maybe I'll become a doctor and find a cure for cancer or win the Nobel Peace Prize or write poetry."

"We're going to miss you so much," said Georgia, and a big tear plopped down her cheek.

"I think you're being very brave," said Olivia.

"Me too," said Tom.

"Stop it," said Aeysha, "or you'll make me cry too." She hugged Georgia. "You are silly. We've still got two whole terms together. Let's enjoy it. Every second."

Chapter Thirty-Five

Eel stepped out on to the ice and promptly fell over.

"It's exceptionally slippery," she said with such surprised indignation that it made the others laugh.

"It's supposed to be slippery, Eel," said Aeysha.

"I know that," said Eel even more indignantly. "It's just. . ." and she sighed sadly, ". . . there's a big gap between how well I think I can skate and how well I can actually skate. It's extremely disappointing."

"Theo's surprisingly good, isn't he, and Kasha's brill," said Katie, watching them both speed-skate across the rink like big kids, chased by a gaggle of squealing younger Swans.

"This is such fun," said Georgia. She turned to Aeysha and Katie. "Shall we skate?" she asked. Aeysha and Katie linked arms with her and the three of them skated away, chatting excitedly to each other.

"It's magical," said Olivia, watching the skaters as they moved in circles around the rink against the glow of a backlit Somerset House. The odd curl of snow fell gently like a feather from a sky pinpricked with tiny stars. It reminded Olivia of the roof of a circus big top.

"It's like something out of a fairytale," agreed Tom. "It's almost impossible to believe that we're right in the heart of London." A conga was starting to form.

"Katie! Katie!" called Kylie. "Join on the back." Katie, followed by Georgia and Aeysha, skated over and caught Kylie by the waist, and the snake moved off, laughing. Kylie and Katie were talking excitedly to each other. Olivia and Tom stood watching them.

"Liv," said Tom seriously. "When you're at Campion's do you still hear the sound of children laughing?"

Olivia blushed. "I'll tell you, as long as you don't call me mad."

"So does that mean yes?" asked Tom.

"Yes, but they're getting fainter every day we are there rehearsing *Cinderella*. Ella's right. They are getting ready to move out." She grinned at Tom. "Come on, I'll race you. The last one to do two full circuits has to buy the roasted chestnuts and mulled apple juice."

Kasha skated over to Georgia and Katie, grinning. "How's the princess?" he asked. Georgia blushed, and Kasha reached out and gently brushed a snowflake from her cheek. Then he caught sight of Abbie talking intently to Alicia by the side of the rink and skated off again in their direction. Georgia stared after him. She sneezed several times as if Kasha touching her cheek had brought on an allergic reaction.

"I need a tissue," she said.

"There's one in my coat pocket. It's over there. The blue one on the top of the pile," said Katie. "Shall I get it for you?"

"I'll go," said Georgia, and she skated off, noticing a number of Swans gathering around Abbie, who was excitedly telling them something. Katie's mum skated by with Jon and waved at her. Georgia waved back. She walked gingerly off the ice and went to Katie's coat. She felt in the pocket for the tissue and as she pulled it out, a cream envelope fell on to the ground.

She picked it up to stuff it back into the coat pocket and as she did so she noticed the name *Kate Carmichael* written on the front. Georgia began to tremble. She suddenly remembered the very first day of the Zelda auditions and seeing a girl in the café whom she had been certain was Katie. So she'd been right! Fury began to rise in her throat. Katie was going to be Zelda. She had got the part, the part that should have been hers. Georgia felt as if her blood was boiling in her veins. She swung round. Katie was spinning in the middle of the rink with Kylie Morris. She looked down at the envelope again and took a step towards the rink, then a quiet voice spoke from behind her.

"Georgia, can I have a word?" Alicia eyes flicked over the envelope and then she studied Georgia's face and said, "We all do things we're ashamed of; we all make mistakes. Sometimes it feels as if life is *forcing* us to make those mistakes. But the mistakes don't matter as long as we do the right thing in the end."

"But . . . but. . ." stuttered Georgia.

"Have you never done anything that you

regret, Georgia, something that makes you feel ashamed to even think about it?" The memory of deleting Poppet's text in the girls' cloakroom popped into Georgia's head.

"Is Katie playing Zelda?" she whispered.

"No," said Alicia, "because Katie thought hard about her options and made her choice, as I hope you will, Georgia. Life is good, isn't it? Why hanker after something you can't have, when you've already got so much that so many would envy?"

Alicia walked slowly away, leaning on her stick. Georgia looked out over the ice. Katie gave her a happy little wave and Kasha beckoned to her. Georgia stuffed the envelope back in Katie's coat and walked back towards the rink. She stepped on to the ice and started skating towards her friends. As she drew level, Aeysha, Olivia, Tom and Eel all raced up to her.

"You'll never guess what!" cried Aeysha. "The most astonishing thing. Abbie has just told us. She met a friend who knew all about it."

"All about what?" demanded Georgia.

"Kylight Productions. Apparently it's gone bust. Something to do with a black hole in the accounts that nobody knew about. The

Zelda movie has been shelved. After all that, *nobody* is going to play Zelda!"

Aeysha drew breath. "We've had a lucky escape, Georgie. Think how awful you'd feel if you'd got the role and then had it snatched away from you like that. It would be awful. I feel really sorry for that poor Kate Carmichael. She must be completely devastated."

"I expect she'll cope," said Katie quietly, but the others didn't hear her because they were all talking excitedly to Kasha, who had joined them. They moved off with him, all except Georgia. She looked hard at Katie. "Of course, maybe she'd already turned it down," she said softly.

Katie swallowed hard. She knew this was treacherous territory, that she and Georgia were skating on very thin ice.

"Yes," said Katie. "I think she had. I think she knew she'd made a terrible mistake by adding her name to the audition list at a time in her life when everything seemed hopeless."

"Carmichael," said Georgia to Katie under her breath. "Same as your mum's name." There was no malice in her voice.

"Yes," said Katie, and she held Georgia's

gaze. "I could tell you all about it if you like. No excuses. Just the truth, warts and all."

"One day that would be nice," said Georgia. "But not yet; it's too soon." She put out her arm towards Katie as if it was an olive branch. "Let's skate."

Chapter Thirty-Six

"He's behind you!"

"Oh no, he's not!" shouted Baron Hard-Up.

"Oh yes, he is!" roared back the delighted audience.

"Oh no, he's not," yelled the baron happily.

"Oh yes, he is," cried the audience at the tops of their voices, so loudly that the crystal drops on Campion's chandelier began to tinkle against each other with the vibrations.

"Oh no, he's—" Theo never delivered the word "not" because a huge custard pie hit him full in the face. The audience stamped and cheered with pleasure. Some even rose to their feet, wild with excitement. As their noise died away, Theo wiped the remains of the pie off his face and with consummate comic timing ad-libbed ruefully, "Maybe he was behind me after all. I should have listened to you." He looked so comically downcast that the audience cracked up all over again.

Standing in the wings watching, Olivia and Tom grinned at each other. The official opening night of the Swan panto was turning into one of the most magical first nights there had ever been in the whole history of London theatre.

Campion's looked like something out of a fairytale. It had been snowing heavily as the audience picked their way down Hangman's Alley and the scene was starting to resemble a Christmas card. Katie's mum had arranged lanterns with flickering fairy lights all the way down the edge of the alleyway, so that the arriving audience walked down a snowy carpet lit by an eerie glow as they headed towards the welcoming pool of warm yellow light that was spilling out from Campion's entrance. There were wreaths made out of holly stuck to all the boarded-up buildings and Alicia had drafted in some of the younger Swans, who didn't have parts in the panto, and dressed them up as cheeky Victorian urchins and matchgirls. At the far end of the alley, by a huge snowman with a carrot nose and skewed top hat, the Swan choir was singing carols. "Silent Night" drifted enchantingly on the breeze, mingling with the flakes of snow that danced downwards from the sky and kissed the arriving audience so that their hair and eyelashes glistened as if dusted with glitter.

Arriving at the ornate entrance, open for the first time in over fifty years, the audience cooed over the plaster vines, stamped the snow from their boots and gasped as they discovered the building's haunting faded grandeur and ruined beauty. The beguiling smell of mulled wine, hot mince pies and roasted chestnuts drifted from the packed bar upstairs down a wooden staircase garlanded with fairy lights. Journalists and critics were gabbling into their mobile phones and demanding that their editors send photographers down to Campion's immediately. One of the curators from the Victoria & Albert Museum was giving a TV interview in front of the exquisitely decorated Christmas tree that stood by the entrance to the auditorium, declaring loudly that Campion's Palace of Varieties was a lost gem that would prove to be one of the most important architectural rediscoveries of the twenty-first century.

"We must preserve it for future generations," the curator declared loudly to the camera, to which Ella, who was standing nearby, snorted, "Preserve it! It's not a pickled onion. It's a theatre. We must use it, let it live and breathe again. It needs new audiences, new ghosts."

But if the theatre-goers were amazed by their journey into the building, it was nothing to their astonishment when they set eyes on the auditorium for the very first time. They gasped out loud at the dazzling beauty of the chandelier with its hundreds of crystal teardrops and couldn't stop touching the twisted candy cane pillars that seemed too delicate and fragile to take the weight of the ornate horseshoe balcony. They were so enchanted by everything they saw that it took a long while for them to settle even as the lights began to dim and the orchestra struck up.

"Here we go," said Theo to all the Swans backstage. "Break a leg, everyone. Let's make a little magic."

Theo was really enjoying himself. He'd never had so much positive publicity. Everyone wanted to interview him and tell the story of the actor who had turned his back on Hollywood for a charity pantomime and a chance to tap dance. It was just as well, he thought ruefully, as he needed a new agent; he and Sheridan had parted company permanently.

Kasha had been in several magazines too, and one of the big Sunday papers had printed a picture of him, Georgia and Abbie under the headline: "The Stars of Tomorrow." Georgia had been speechless with pleasure, and Aeysha, Olivia and Tom had teased her mercilessly about it, which Georgia had taken with the good grace of someone who knew she was having her little patch of sunlight.

"It might not last, so I'm going to enjoy every minute of it while it does," she said.

"The funny thing is," said Aeysha, "that I'm enjoying you enjoying it."

"Yes," said Katie wonderingly. "It's as if Georgia's success feels like all our success." She looked puzzled. "Once I wouldn't have thought that possible. I would have been raging inside that it should have been me."

"Maybe it will be you one day, Katie," Georgia had murmured softly. She had a feeling that she and Katie were going to be good friends.

The overture reached a dramatic climax and the false safety curtain – decorated with a wonderful image of Victorian skaters against a London skyline, which Katie's mum had made to go in front of the Campion's stage – began to rise. As it did so, all that the audience could see at first was a chorus line of feet all tapping away furiously. The noise was like a thunderstorm of hailstones; the energy and exhilaration it generated could have launched a rocket into space. The audience broke into excited spontaneous applause. The curtain rose a little higher to reveal three lines of Swans all tap dancing furiously. Right in the centre of the front row was Theo, a vast grin of happiness lighting up his face. Behind him a pantomime horse attempted and repeatedly failed to copy what he was doing. For what would be the first of many times that night, the audience rose to their feet in rapturous applause.

Chapter Thirty-Seven

By the interval, it was clear that it wasn't just Campion's that was a complete triumph; the Swan panto was a huge hit too. Several camera crews had arrived outside the theatre. More and more journalists had got wind that a story was unfolding and were trying to crowd into the back of the balcony.

"It's a complete sell-out," said Georgia happily as she lifted her face during the interval and allowed Katie to reapply the make-up that had started to run under the hot lights.

"Not quite full," said Eel. "Emmy and I spotted three empty seats right in the middle of the front of the balcony. Somebody can't have showed up. They'll be mad when they realise what they've missed."

"I heard that Ella wouldn't sell those seats," said Aeysha. "She wanted to keep them free. But the really odd thing is it's not just for tonight. She doesn't want them sold for any of the performances."

"But why would anyone keep three seats free in a completely sold-out theatre?" asked Eel. "It's like laying extra places for every meal just in case some unexpected guests turn up."

Olivia said nothing, but she felt certain she knew who those seats were being kept for.

By the time the second half was underway, the audience was breaking into spontaneous applause every few minutes, and at one point after a breathless tap-dancing display by Theo the entire audience had stood up and stopped the show for several minutes.

"I love this," said Theo happily as he rushed into the wings. Olivia smiled at him. The panto horse had gone down a storm too. Particularly when the two of them had got up on the high-wire and done a little comedy routine in which the front feet and the back feet of the horses were entirely at odds with each other.

The show was nearing its end. The prince had been reunited with his princess. The marriage was about to take place. Only the final long segment of the panto – which was called the walk-down – remained. Olivia and Tom were standing in the wings, watching. They had got so adept at getting their costume on and off that they always waited until the final moment to put it on, otherwise it got so hot inside it felt as if they were in a sauna. On the other side of the stage Ella was standing watching too.

The Swans were dancing and singing their hearts out. Katie and Kylie were swinging each other round, a look of pure pleasure on their faces. Georgia had just arrived in the wings wearing her wedding gown. The dress sparkled, but it was Georgia's face that gave off a thousand volts of happiness. Olivia caught several of the older boys glancing at Georgia admiringly, as if they had suddenly noticed her for the first time.

Olivia suddenly saw Ella look out from the wings into the auditorium and up towards the balcony. Her mouth was a little circle of surprise and her eyes were shining. Her hand was raised as if she was making a gesture that could have been a wave and could have been a blessing. She was obviously watching somebody and she was enraptured. Olivia's eyes followed Ella's gaze to the front row of the balcony. For a moment she could see nothing, but as her eyes adjusted she spotted them: a boy, a girl and a woman dressed in the fashions of the nineteen fifties making their way along the front row towards the exit. Olivia glanced hurriedly around. Nobody else on stage or in the audience seemed to have noticed the children and their mother. Nobody could see them except her and Ella. At the exit, the children suddenly threw back their heads and roared with laughter, waved at Ella and Olivia, blew them both a kiss and disappeared. Above the music, Olivia could hear a single word: "Thank you."

Olivia looked back at Ella. Tears were pouring down her cheeks but she was smiling. Arthur appeared as if from nowhere and squeezed her hand. "I saw them," she whispered to him. "They've forgiven me. They let me say goodbye." Arthur looked lovingly at her, then he cupped her face gently in both his hands and kissed her softly on the lips.

"Did you see that?" Tom asked Olivia.

"Yes," said Olivia happily.

"It's funny," whispered Tom as he helped Olivia into their costume. "I can't imagine why I ever thought Campion's was spooky. It feels like the friendliest and happiest place in the whole world tonight."

"That's because the ghosts have got what they wanted. Campion's is open for business again. They can rest now," said Olivia.

"Ready?" asked Tom.

"Ready for anything," said Olivia. The great chandelier suddenly sparked into life as Georgia and Kasha made their entrance, the orchestra music swelled and Campion's was lit up in all its glory like an exquisite mirrored chocolate box. The crowd went crazy.

"Let's go," said Tom, and they galloped on to the stage behind the happy couple. Olivia listened very hard. The only sound she could hear was the audience clapping and cheering. She knew for certain that Campion's ghosts had made their final exit.

The entire cast crowded on to the stage. Ella and Arthur were lost somewhere in the throng but they really only had eyes for each other. Jon and Katie's mum had joined the cast on stage after the persistent calls from the audience for "director" and "designer". Katie saw her mum's shining face and her own eyes welled with tears. Kylie noticed, and quickly put her arm around her. Aeysha smiled and smiled and thought how much she would miss this when she didn't perform any more, and how she was going to squeeze every second of pleasure from it while she still did.

Kasha leaned towards Georgia to give her one last kiss and the audience heaved a collective sigh of pleasure. Jon signalled to the orchestra to begin playing "We Wish You a Merry Christmas" and the whole cast linked arms and began to sing.

"This," said Theo, grinning wildly and breaking into a spontaneous shuffle, "is quite simply one of the best nights of my life."

"And it's just about to get better," said Olivia, looking upwards.

From high up in the ceiling thousands of fake snowflakes begun to swirl and fall. The audience and Swans reached out their hands delightedly to catch the whirling flakes. The sound of their laughter was so loud that it spilled beyond the walls of Campion's Palace of Varieties and out into the snowy, silent streets, and was carried on the wind across the glittering city.